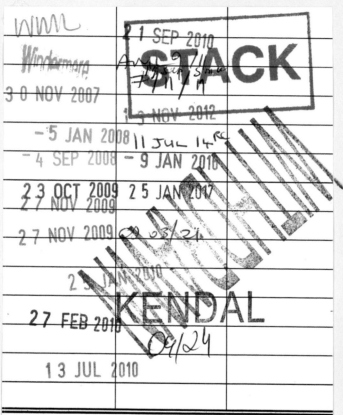

Born and raised in New Hampshire, Elisabeth Hyde has since lived in Vermont, Washington D.C., San Francisco and Seattle. In 1979 she received her law degree and practised briefly with the U.S. Department of Justice. She teaches creative writing and currently lives with her husband and three children in Boulder, Colorado, where she is at work on her next novel.

CRAZY AS CHOCOLATE

Ellie and Izzy have lived a life with a mother they adored. Whether taking them for long midnight baths or dancing in the dark in the rain, she's been a magical, colourful figure. Now, on the eve of her forty-first birthday, Izzy realizes that she's about to reach the year her mother never got beyond. Her father and sister are flying out for an emotionally charged weekend visit, and Izzy can't help feeling that she's still responsible, that there are apologies to be made. Surely now she's at an age where a grown-up daughter can put things behind her?

Books by Elisabeth Hyde
Published by The House of Ulverscroft:

THE ABORTIONIST'S DAUGHTER

ELISABETH HYDE

CRAZY AS CHOCOLATE

Complete and Unabridged

CHARNWOOD
Leicester

First published in Great Britain in 2007 by
Pan Books
an imprint of
Pan Macmillan Limited, London

First Charnwood Edition
published 2007
by arrangement with
Pan Macmillan Limited, London

British Library CIP Data

Hyde, Elisabeth
    Crazy as chocolate.—Large print ed.—
    Charnwood library series
    1. Suicide victims—Family relationships—Fiction
    2. Mothers and daughters—Fiction
    3. Mothers—Death—Fiction 4. Large type books
    I. Title
    813.5'4 [F]

    ISBN 978–1–84617–959–4

Published by
F. A. Thorpe (Publishing)
Anstey, Leicestershire

Set by Words & Graphics Ltd.
Anstey, Leicestershire
Printed and bound in Great Britain by
T. J. International Ltd., Padstow, Cornwall

This book is printed on acid-free paper

*Even crazy, I'm as nice
as a chocolate bar.*

— Anne Sexton

For my daughters, Kate and Zoe

1

When I went off to college, I started telling people that my mother died in a car crash. Lying comes easy when you're raised by a liar. I said it happened long ago, when I was very young, and I always added that she died instantly and did not suffer. It was something I could easily imagine my father saying to a small child, to comfort her. Hearing this, people felt bad, but at least they knew what to say. When people learn the truth, they're always at a loss.

I even kept my husband in the dark for a long time, although to make up for the lie, I told him many things that were true. I told him, for instance, how my father did a good job raising my sister Ellie and me — how he cooked oatmeal every morning and monitored our homework and shamed us for throwing away our sandwich crusts. I told him how we got to take dance lessons and go to sleepover camp; how we squabbled over whose turn it was to set the table, or who got which Beatle to be in love with. True things, normal little things, as though we were a normal little family.

But after telling him all this, I summed things up by saying that, all things considered, I had a happy childhood. And when he found out the truth he felt a deeper betrayal than I had anticipated.

What did you think I'd do, Isabel? he asked. Walk?

★　★　★

Truth, exaggeration, embellishment: my mother had problems distinguishing these concepts. A woman taken with large numbers, she once tried to explain how small a molecule was. There are more molecules in a grain of sand, she told Ellie and me, than there are grains of sand in the world. It was her effort at truth, I guess, and yet as a child I found the concept hard to believe. I thought of beaches and sand dunes, I thought of the Great Sahara Desert and I wanted to say to my mother: This can't be true; you're exaggerating again.

I'll never know what triggered things for her, in the end. Or what exactly was wrong. Maybe there was an umbrella diagnosis back then that covered all her symptoms, but as to where the doctors might pigeonhole her today, I don't know. Nor will I know what caused her to unravel in the first place. Sometimes I think it was some grave parenting error on Nana's part. Other times I'm convinced it was just in her genes, a matter of time before she finally descended into that long, loopy downward spiral.

What I do know is that I loved her. She tried to be a good mother, in spite of everything.

Tomorrow I turn forty-one. When my mother turned forty-one, in March of 1971, she locked herself in the garage and sat in a Dodge Dart with the engine running. Since then, I have spent each and every anniversary of her death with a case of emotional hiccups, getting through maybe all of thirty seconds before I flash once again on my father dragging her out of the garage, or the paramedics draping her with a sheet, or the white camellia blossoms in the dark mist. My own birthday in September was never a worry, because it's at the opposite time of year, when the light is brittle and bright and the weather is hot and there are no memories floating around.

Then last month, as I stood in line to renew my driver's license, it struck me I was about to enter virgin time, the second half of a life unlived, a life my mother never knew. I began to dread the birthday — not the years to follow, just the day itself. I made a plan: no party, no surprises, just my husband Gabe and me. We would hike the Mesa trail at the base of the Flatirons, among the dry, open Ponderosa that are so unlike the dark, damp, decaying forests in the Pacific Northwest, where I grew up. All I wanted from my father was a phone call, maybe a long-distance Are you doing okay, hang in there honey. And all I wanted from Ellie (who's forty-three and should have warned me) was a simple Happy Birthday from one sane sister to another.

Two days ago, however, my father called and announced they'd both be flying out for the birthday weekend — he from Seattle, Ellie from New York. I protested, but he wouldn't listen. He said my birthday was a good excuse for us all to get together, and besides, the tickets were nonrefundable. Because he could guess what I was thinking, he offered a kind of solace. He said the age shouldn't mean anything, because my mother wasn't all there for many, many years before the actual end. I might as well have chosen my thirty-sixth birthday to get spooked by, he said, as she was thirty-six the first time she tried to kill herself. Or my thirty-eighth birthday, since that was the year she stopped taking all her medications. You're turning forty-one, he said. But you're not your mother. You have the rest of your life to live. Live it for yourself.

And I said, You're right. Nevertheless, the small dark animal that clamped itself around my heart twenty-eight years ago dug its claws a little deeper. I still miss her like it happened yesterday. I still feel responsible, still feel there are apologies to be made. And if forty-one is anything, it's an age where a grown daughter ought to be able to put these things behind her.

★ ★ ★

Heatwise it's been a bitch of a summer here in Colorado. I have eaten more salads than I care to contemplate, I sleep naked, I keep the swamp cooler on and the fans blowing all night long and still I wake up every morning to a hot blast pouring in from the eastern plains. At seven o'clock tonight, the thermometer reads ninety-four in the shade, and don't let anyone tell you that dry western heat doesn't feel hot. It feels as hot as Africa, to me.

Marriage-wise, it's been a hard summer, too. Gabe and I have been married for thirteen years, but much of that time has been spent trying without success to have a child. It'll do it to the strongest of couples — temperature taking, scheduled sex, month after month until you both go in for tests and you get ink blown up your tubes and he gets his sperm count tested, both of you pass and then it's on to injections and hormones and still the basal body temperature keeps falling every month. Last winter Gabe suddenly found himself unable to get an erection whenever I was ovulating — all I had to do was remark that it was Day Thirteen and he'd start sleeping in pajamas. In response, I began to accuse him of not really wanting a child, and in his meaner moments he'd raise the genetic issue, by which he meant my mother, and by April we'd not only given up on the whole wretched pregnancy quest but decided that maybe a little time apart would be good for us.

So as of June first, Gabe took a summer sublet in town. I spent my summer nights in a hot empty bed. When his lease came up at the end of August, we took a long walk up into the canyon and came back having decided three things: one, we didn't want to keep living apart; two, there ought to be more to our marriage than successful cell division; and three, if we really wanted a baby it was time to stop piddling around with the adoption idea and get our names on a list.

So Gabe moved back a few weeks ago. (I never mentioned any of this to my father or my sister, and no doubt I will pay a price with Ellie, who expects full disclosure on everything.) And things seem to be on an upswing — which is remarkable, given my bitchiness in the current heat wave. We kiss each other hello and goodbye, and use each other's name, and are quick to apologize for the smallest transgression. We've even made love a lot, and I'm proud to say I've gotten right up afterward instead of lying there with my knees drawn up, the way I used to, in order to give all those spermatozoa the downhill advantage.

Now it's Friday night and Gabe is rooting around in the refrigerator, threatening to cook despite the heat. Gabe and I met in law school, in Trusts and Estates to be precise, but Gabe was never cut out to be a lawyer because he shies away from confrontation and in fact would rather be scaling a two-thousand-foot cliff than facing down an opponent in court. This passion for heights, combined with a basic instinct for business, led him to open a hang-gliding and paragliding school here in Colorado. These days he teaches the sport to mostly middle-aged men in search of risk. After one day of ground handling, he takes them to the top of the rocky cliffs north of town, tells them their risk of dying is one in a thousand, and pushes them off, a culminating act of aggression for which they happily shell out a week's salary.

White mist swirls into his face as he opens the freezer door. 'What's this?' he says, pulling out a package of meat. 'Pork tenderloin, it looks like — how about I marinate it?'

6

'Gabe,' I say, 'I'm sorry but if you cook I will puke.'

Gabe sweats easily, and doesn't understand how the heat can bother someone. He tells me to pretend it's winter and I've been stuck in a blizzard all night and have just this very moment stepped into a sauna. Under less testing circumstances I would tell him to shut up. As it is, I remind him that he has offered this image before, and it doesn't work.

Gabe must have detected something in my voice, because after he puts the meat in the microwave, he gets two beers from the refrigerator. 'Bad day?'

I haven't told him this, but I have an ugly case right now where the grandparents are seeking custody of their grandchild, a ten-year-old girl whose mother stays locked in her room because she is one hundred percent convinced she is going to poison her daughter: She might mix ammonia with bleach, say, or give her the wrong Tylenol, or too much cough syrup. When she isn't locked in her room, she's threatening to drive her car off Flagstaff Mountain. You'd think it'd be a clear-cut case, but the mother claims she's just being prudent, and regarding the comments about Flagstaff Mountain, she would never in a million years take her life. Next week I have to take her deposition, and I am afraid that she, like my mother, will be as charming as she is crazy.

I can be as gullible as a child, when face to face with madness.

The cold beer tastes bitter and slightly sweet. I

find that if I raise my arms at just the right angle, the table fan blows straight into the valley between my breasts. I don't really want to delve into the grandparents' case right now.

'I thought you had a class tonight,' I say.

'No wind.'

'Ten to one Ellie will want to go hang gliding,' I venture. My sister learned to hang glide in France, two years ago. 'Will you take her?'

'Depends on whether she's gained some weight. I don't want her to float away.'

His joke about my sister's quasi-anorexic state puts me on the defensive. I can criticize my family, but he can't. As he douses the meat with soy sauce, I point out that he is going to heat up the entire house just to cook a pound of meat.

'I'm using the grill,' he reminds me.

'So? The heat will blow right into the house.'

'Isabel,' my husband says, 'this is summer in America. And what do people do when it's summer in America? They fire up the grill. Now go take a shower. Take a cold shower. Take a long, cold shower, drink another beer, and go naked.'

'How am I going to be nice this weekend, when it's ninety-eight degrees?' I ask. 'I really think this is not a good idea.'

'Well, nobody ever said life was fair,' Gabe tells me, as though it's the wisest thing in the world.

★ ★ ★

Here's my shower routine: soap up, check for lumps, rinse, shave, check for lumps, touch my

8

toes, squeak my hair, check for lumps.

My mother taught me.

I don't know, Gabe, am I crazy?

I haven't seen my father in a year, Ellie in ten months. My prediction is that my father, who is seventy-one, will have lost no hair and gained no weight, and he will be wearing the same pair of chinos and blue button-down shirt that he always travels in. A dandy, my father is not. Ellie, though — well, who knows what Ellie will have done to herself.

Married to a man named Wilson whose exact business eludes everyone, Ellie lives half the year on Park Avenue and half the year in Cannes. As far back as I can remember, she has displayed a propensity for change; over the years she has worn her hair long, short, shaved, permed, corn-rowed, and dredlocked. She also has an affinity for body piercing and discreet tattoos. I have no idea what to expect, except that she'll be wearing black, that being the only color she ever wears.

And Ellie may or may not bring her daughter Rachel, who is seven. Rachel is my goddaughter. I was there for her birth, and held her when she was five minutes old while Wilson, drunk and giddy from the success of Ellie's thirty-five-hour labor, exuberantly tried to make out with her. Somewhere, sometime, there was a redhead in someone's family, because Rachel's hair is the color of an Irish setter's fur, naturally curly, with dizzy ringlets falling every which way. She wants to be a boy when she grows up.

The shower cools me off, and I put on a short,
loose linen dress and join Gabe by the grill,
where he is scraping off charred bits of some
kind of flesh from last spring.

'Who-all is showing up tomorrow?' he asks.

'Dad and Ellie. Maybe Rachel.'

'What about Wilson?'

'I don't know.'

'Is it just me or is Ellie really a lot calmer
when he's around?'

'She'll be herself, whether he's here or not.'

'She can't smoke here,' he reminds me. 'Not
even outside.'

'She knows that.'

Gabe bastes the meat with a dark liquid. 'Not
to bring up ancient history, but is she still
pushing the egg thing?'

I had a feeling he would raise this issue. Like
me, Ellie found it difficult to get pregnant. But
she started earlier, and eight years ago, while
undergoing fertility treatments, she froze a few
extra eggs, thinking they might come in handy at
some later date. Since then, she has decided
against having another child, but frozen eggs
can't just go to waste, and about a year ago,
while I was visiting her in New York, she offered
them to me.

I said no. While a part of me could have
borrowed my sister's eggs as easily as I might
have borrowed a sweater, there were good
reasons to decline the offer. For one thing, I had
my doubts that Ellie would be able to relinquish

her claim on any child that might have been born. And as I found out when I got home, Gabe was dead set against the idea, convinced as he was that Ellie's eggs contained the crazy gene from our mother — the CR001, he calls it, a typo on the double helix. This rankled me, because this crazy gene could have been lurking in his genealogy too. I wasn't wild about the idea myself, and I let the matter drop. He was never going to change his mind. My husband doesn't get to call all the shots, but I respect how he feels, which seems like the right thing to do in any marriage.

And the issue's moot now, since we're no longer trying. I don't remind Gabe of this, but merely tell him that no, Ellie hasn't mentioned her eggs lately.

'Good. And I hope she doesn't ask me all that stuff about my brother, either.' Gabe had an older brother who died in Vietnam. Every time we get together Ellie probes into this area — when Gabe last saw him, and what it was like when they got the notice, and whether Gabe himself feels guilty for not having served. This is stuff Gabe doesn't really like to talk about, not even with me, and I learned long ago not to press. But Ellie does, and that bugs him.

I glance at him as he stands at the grill, one hand on his hip, the other tonging the meat. He is a tall man, with a chiseled jaw, a heavy beard, and a high, sloping forehead. His eyes are the color of molasses, and in his left iris there is a golden fleck shaped like the continent of Africa which disappears when he gets mad. His light

11

brown hair is fine and straight, and tends to fly off in all directions when he wakes up each morning. The diamond in his left ear is new.

'Just tell her you don't want to talk about your brother,' I say. 'She won't bite.' Heat ripples up from the grill. There is no escape. In a few years I could get hot flashes, and then what will I do?

Here's what my mother never experienced: menopause.

'Oh, Ellie bites,' he says. 'Don't deny that.'

'Still. Be nice to her.'

'I'm very nice,' he says.

'Be nice to everyone.'

'This isn't what either of us wanted for the weekend,' he reminds me.

'No,' I say, 'but it's what's going to happen. Please be nice.'

'I'm very nice,' he says.

2

My mother grew up in the White Mountains of New Hampshire. She used to tell Ellie and me about climbing to the top of Mount Lafayette, crossing great barren avalanche gullies and scrambling over rocks and finally standing tall at the highest point, gazing away to the state of Maine and the Atlantic Ocean beyond. Ellie and I didn't believe her. It was not possible, we maintained, to stand in the middle of one state and see across another. Where we came from, states were large, and mountain ranges vast, and you could not stand in the middle of Washington and see all the way to Idaho. My mother would add that she'd been able to see not only the state of Maine but the state of Vermont as well. She would get out a map to show us how small the states were back in New England, and I would be convinced, although Ellie maintained that my mother was telling another one of her stories.

Having grown up in the mountains, the first thing she wanted to do when she moved to Seattle was to climb Mount Rainier. To her credit she managed to climb it twice before Ellie and I were born. After that my father convinced her that motherhood didn't mesh with high-altitude climbing, so she limited herself to short hikes with us in the meadows near the old Paradise Lodge. We would feed our sandwiches to the birds, and search the snow fields above for hikers. If we were lucky we would see a group nearing the summit, a string of commas bent against the wind.

Once my mother took us up into the snow fields. I was nine and Ellie was eleven and we were not yet ready to attempt the overnight trek to the summit. For that kind of a climb, you needed stamina, which we had, but you also needed the strength to carry food, and water, and a sleeping bag and extra clothing and ropes and cleats and an ice ax and a hard-hat for the place where the rocks came tumbling down on your head. We were not ready for that, my mother said, and so we planned a hike to Tower Rock, where summit-bound hikers spent the night.

Of course, we got lost. My mother wanted to eat lunch away from other hikers, and she said she knew of a ledge with a good view of Mount Saint Helens, which had not at that point erupted. She led us away from the trail and across the snow field, and down a ravine and up again, and then she said she guessed maybe the ledge was on the other side of the trail. We tried to go back but instead of the ravine there was a rocky gorge in our way. In minutes the terrain had lost all familiarity.

'Oh, pooh,' my mother said. 'Darn it all.'

Ellie and I looked at each other. This was typical of my mother, to get us lost like this.

'Don't look at me,' my mother said defensively, shading her eyes. 'It wasn't there two minutes ago, that gorge. Was it? Come on, was it? I don't think so.'

14

She sat down on a bit of exposed rock and lit a cigarette. She was wearing an old army parka of my father's, drab green and frayed at the edges, onto which she had sewn embroidered ribbon around the hood and cuffs, so she looked like some kind of a post-war hausfrau making do with the discards. As she smoked, she hugged her knees and told us of the time she and our father had gone skinny-dipping in the surf on the Oregon coast. 'And whose idea was it?' she demanded. 'Mine, thank you. Your father is so modest. Not that anyone would have minded, the way he's built.'

Ellie said something unintelligible to the sky.

'Don't whine,' my mother said. 'Really, Ellie, you're eleven years old and you still whine like you were two. Anyway,' she continued, 'afterward I wanted to make love on the beach but your father said it would be too cold. In fact he was just being a priss. Your father can really be a priss, you know.'

'We're lost,' Ellie said. 'We're going to freeze to death, and you're telling us stories about sex on a cold beach? Are you crazy?'

'I don't know,' my mother said calmly, and she turned to me. 'Am I crazy, Izzy?'

'No,' I lied.

'I don't think I'm crazy,' my mother remarked.

'Is that a light?' Ellie said.

I looked where Ellie was looking, but saw nothing except the black rocks of the gorge. There had been no sunset — it was too cloudy for that — but the sun was long gone, and the light was dim. Above us loomed the mountain,

15

cold and gray. Up close like this, it appeared much smaller, like a large hill of snow that we could scoot up and slide down in an hour or two.

'There!' Ellie exclaimed. 'See it?'

Across the gorge a faint light bobbed in the dusk. I sighed inwardly with relief — not because we were going to get rescued, but because my mother would have to stop talking about sex. Ellie and I climbed up on the rock and jumped up and down and yelled as hard as we could. As the light bobbed in our direction, my mother stopped talking about the Oregon coast and we all began to plan what we would have for dinner when we got back to civilization. Ellie and I wanted hamburgers and Cokes, my mother wanted a Denver omelet and a beer. We all wanted a bath and it was decided that I would get the first one because I was the thinnest and therefore probably the coldest. Ellie wasn't much fatter, but she could be a good older sister if she chose.

The search party — my father must have phoned when we failed to arrive home for dinner — consisted of two young rangers. My mother flirted with them, and managed to learn very quickly that one was from Yale and the other was from the University of Texas, and that they were out here for the summer. The one from Yale was pre-med and the one from the University of Texas didn't know what his major would be. My mother, suddenly his guidance counselor, said that was all right, he had plenty of time. They looked impatient and asked my mother why we had ventured over here, far away from the trail.

No extra clothing, no food, no water — what had gotten into us? They tried to be polite but you could tell they thought we were stupid city people.

By the time we got back to the car, it was nine-thirty. After calling my father, we drove quickly down the mountain and stopped for food at the first place we found open, a roadhouse built of logs and shakes, with weedy flower boxes in the windows and a lone gas pump in the parking lot. The restaurant was empty and quiet, save for the bubbling hum of an orangeade cooler on the counter.

'Yoo hoo,' my mother called out. I wanted to die, she sounded so goofy. And when a large man in a plaid shirt came out to say they were closed, she made things worse by embellishing our story with frostbite and dehydration and hypothermia, afterward falling into a fit of coughing, keeping her hand over her mouth and then, when she was through, checking it for blood. She'd read a news article about tuberculosis that week.

'I guess we could cook you some hamburgers,' the man said. 'Joyce!' he called out. 'Joyce'll get you some hamburgers. You need some blankets? Cocoa?'

'Aren't you a sweetheart,' my mother said.

Joyce came over and set our table. The placemats had a map of Washington, illustrated with little apples and salmon and totem poles. Ellie was a doodler, and she took out a pencil and laced all the apples together up and down the Okanogan Valley. My mother smoked a cigarette, and I flipped through the jukebox cards until my mother gave me a dime. I chose the Beatles; I was in love with John.

On the way back, Ellie sat up front and I lay down across the back seat, watching the stars. My mother turned the radio on and we all just rode together, listening to the Bee Gees, and the Turtles, and the Fifth Dimension. Occasionally my mother joined in with a refrain, bopping her head back and forth as she gripped the steering wheel. This would draw Ellie from some private reverie, and my mother would laugh outright, girlishly, and Ellie, who was trying to stay dour, would finally allow the teeniest, tiniest little smile. I felt happy and safe.

We got home after midnight. My father was waiting up for us, and he had a few words with my mother, but mostly he was glad to see us back. He kissed us and went upstairs. My mother did not rush us off to bed but gave us ginger ale and Cheez Doodles. Since no one felt tired, she suggested that we all take a bath together. We did this a lot — Ellie had only just started to develop, and it still seemed as natural as eating together. We went upstairs and my mother began filling the bathtub, shaking a bottle of rosemary oil over the water. She closed the door to let the room steam up and we all got undressed and wrapped our heads, turban-style, in white towels. Soon we could hardly see, it was so steamy. Our bathtub was six feet long, and we could all fit by sitting crosswise with our legs draped over the rim: Ellie in the deeper front end, me in the middle with my head right under the soap dish, and my mother at the shallow back end, her right arm draped over the edge. When we thought we couldn't stand the heat any longer, my mother took the bottle of rosemary oil and dabbed a bit beneath our noses. The strong piney scent chilled my nostrils, my throat, and my lungs, like liquid winter.

It was two-thirty before we got to bed that night. My mother made sure that our hair was dry and our teeth had been thoroughly brushed and then insisted, although we were way too old, that she read to us from *A Child's Garden of Verses*. Afterward she tucked us in, gave us a kiss on the forehead, and told us to sleep as late as we could in the morning.

★   ★   ★

That was as close as I ever got to the summit of Mount Rainier. The next year my mother enrolled us all in a mountaineering course, but halfway through she decided that the instructor was coming on to her, and became convinced that his lust would make him soft on us. The year after that, two hikers fell to their deaths and my mother dreamt that the mountain blew up, and she forbade us from going near the mountain. And the year after that was the year she parked the Dodge in the garage with the engine running, and that was the end of everything, for a long time.

That terrible March night, I lay beside Ellie in her bed in the room we shared. The window between our beds was open and the curtains wafted gently. All I could see was darkness. On

19

summer nights we could see Mount Rainier from her bed, and I imagined for a moment it was that time of year, one of the warm iridescent nights on which the mountain would turn color, from white to rose to purplish pink. I pictured the mountain as it appeared to me as a child: a cloud of apple blossoms, or a scoop of ice cream, or part of a pastel mural in a baby's room.

That night, though, nothing was visible. I closed my eyes and tried to pretend what had happened was a bad dream. That everything was all right, really. That a couple of hours ago we'd all cracked lobsters together and my mother blew out the candles on her birthday cake, and was sleeping in the room next to us, alive and normal as everyone else. I imagined being up there on the mountain with my mother and Ellie and my father. I imagined us halfway to the summit, camped for the night. Outside the wind howled and slapped at the walls of our tent, while inside we nestled in our sleeping bags, waiting for dawn. In a few hours my mother would wake us, and lead the way, urging us on to the top, where we would all huddle together, and drink the hot tea my mother would produce from a thermos.

It's how you get through a night like that, when you're twelve and a half.

* * *

Our family, like all families, started out hopeful. My parents loved each other, and we as their children were very much wanted and loved. But by the time my mother succeeded in killing herself, nobody was really, truly surprised. Certainly not my father, and Ellie and I were hardly blind to the demons in her eyes on certain nights.

But knowledge and acceptance are two very different things. If I have a wish right now on the eve of my birthday, it is to go back in time, to say to her loudly and clearly, Don't leave us, it's really, really a mistake, and for her to hear it in her heart, and turn off the ignition.

3

Gabe's piece of meat, together with all that mesquite, produces enough smoke that our neighbor to the west calls the fire department. The long chartreuse truck pulls into our driveway, honking loudly. Gabe runs down the steps and explains things to Sidney, the fire chief. Thankfully, Sid is one of Gabe's best friends, and after explaining the source of the smoke, Gabe invites Sid to share a beer. Now they are down in the driveway, drinking long necks and inspecting the tires on the fire truck.

It's too hot to eat out on the deck, so I go inside to set the table. Our house has an open dining room and living room. The southern wall is mostly glass and overlooks a rocky slope studded with Ponderosa pine. Opposite this wall, on the living room end, stands a large rock fireplace, with bookshelves on either side. Above, in the cathedral loft, Gabe has hung the tattered nylon panels of every flying device he has ever owned. Blue and red and purple and yellow, billowing gently from beam to beam, these orphaned sails give the house the feel of an air and space museum.

The dining room table is strewn with newspapers, mail, and brown accordion files from my office. One of the files belongs to the grandparents in my custody case. They're regular folks; Carl's a mechanic, Wilma's a school-teacher, and they want custody so bad they've already remodeled their house to accommodate their granddaughter — playroom, swingset, Little Tykes house. They know about misfortune — Wilma's gone through chemo and Carl's a Vietnam vet himself — but they tell me nothing compares to filing a lawsuit against your own daughter. It breaks my heart to pieces, Wilma says, but what are we supposed to do? Sit back and wait for a tragedy like that momma who shot her little boy and then herself?

Gabe is calling. I edge open the sliding door and poke my head out, straight into a blast of heat. He wants me to take the meat off the grill. He's pressing his luck here, I think, but I'll cut him some slack. I could use a little practice being nice, because my family will be here in less than twenty-four hours, and the heat still has me as crabby as a substitute teacher. I turn off the grill, raise the cover, bat the smoke, and move the meat off to the side. It looks like a small burnt forearm. I go back inside to where it is so blessedly cool, because it is time to call my sister and double-check on her flight schedule.

As I reach for the phone, though, it burbles and I answer it and it is Ellie, calling from New York to tell me what time her plane gets in. This happens a lot. I'll have a fight with Gabe, and Ellie will call and ask how things are going between the two of us these days. Or I'll get a whopper cold, and she'll call and the first thing she does is apologize for being so stuffed up — it's a bug she picked up at Rachel's school and she just can't seem to shake it.

'Isabella,' she says. 'Everything okay?'

'Everything's fine, except it's hotter'n shit.'

'It's hot everywhere. So, are you flipping out?'

'Over what?'

'Over our coming out! Over the fact that it's a bitch of a birthday, which Dad knows, but he told me we're not going to be around forever, those were his words, and we should enjoy this time together while we can. I thought that was kind of morbid, actually. Tell me the truth. Is Dad sick? Is there something he's not telling me?'

'Not that I know of.'

'So what do you want to do, sweet pea? The weekend's all yours. You know what I did when I turned forty-one?'

'What?'

'I fucked Rachel's teacher. Ha! Just kidding. Though I did think about it. You would not believe this guy, oh my God.'

'What's your point?'

'Isabella,' she says, 'since when do I have to have a point when I'm talking to you?'

I straighten one of Gabe's kachinas on the wall. Gabe has thirty-four of these violent-looking wooden dolls, all adorned with fur and feathers and little axes and arrows and belts. When we had them appraised, we questioned whether we should keep them on the wall or put them in a safety deposit box. Gabe has yet to make up his mind, and in the meantime they glare down upon us every night at dinner. Me, I wouldn't mind selling them and using the money to remodel the kitchen.

'Yoo hoo,' my sister says. 'Are you there?'

I blow dust from a doll's shoulders. 'Is Wilson coming?'

'No,' she says, yawning, 'he's got business.'

'What about Rachel?'

'Of course I'm bringing her! Not that she'll be in the way. She and Dad can go off and play and we can bake gingerbread houses together. Make a fine mess for Gabe to clean up.'

'It's too hot to bake,' I say. 'Listen. Tell me something. Did you feel relieved when it was over? Or free?'

'No,' she says, 'but I felt older than Mom ever felt, and that's a true fact.'

Free is how I want to feel, though. I imagine myself tomorrow evening, the cage door open, one little hop, then glorious flight up through the canopy of trees. This birthday is bothering me a heck of a lot more than I thought it would.

'Aren't we stupid,' I say, 'fixating on something like this.'

'Probably.'

'I mean, it's just a stupid day. There are wars going on. People are dying.'

'Right.'

'How'd you get through it?'

'Mega-drugs,' she says. 'The legal kind.'

'How come Dad didn't schedule a party for you?'

'You're the nice one,' Ellie replies.

This bothers me, since it's true. 'What time do you get in?'

'Three-fifteen. Isabel,' she says, lowering her

voice, 'you're right, you know. It is just a day. You're you. You're not her. Nobody's her. It'll be okay,' she reminds me. 'It's something, but then again it's nothing, really. Just a vacuum bag full of dust.'

'Isn't that Mom's phrase?'

'So sue me for copyright,' says Ellie. 'See you tomorrow.'

Outside, Gabe slaps the hood of the fire truck as Sid backs out of our driveway. He joins me on the deck.

'I just got off the phone with Ellie,' I say. 'Wilson's not coming.'

Gabe makes a face. 'How long are they staying?'

'Until Sunday.'

'This Sunday? Hey, that's not so bad. I thought they were staying for a week.' He lifts the shrunken arm of meat from the grill and sets it on a plate. 'If they're leaving Sunday afternoon, that gives us Sunday night,' he says. 'We'll do something, just the two of us.'

'Sunday seems a long way off right now,' I say glumly.

'Jesus, Isabel,' he says. 'Look, they're going to be here for twenty-four hours. What can happen in twenty-four hours?' He shuts the grill and squints down at the meat.

'This looks awful,' he says.

⋆   ⋆   ⋆

The last time I saw my sister was ten months ago. I had a business trip to New York and

26

figured I could catch my sister right before she and Wilson and Rachel left for their six months in France. I called her from my office and told her I was coming. Ellie said, fine, cool, groovy.

This was no glamour trip. My practice is mostly family law, divorce cases and custody disputes and a bit of estate planning, but one of my clients was selling her apartment in New York and she asked me to handle the closing. I spent the morning on the forty-fifth floor of a mid-town building, watching people sign documents. The air in the room gave me a headache, so after the meeting I walked the thirty-odd blocks up to Ellie's.

For the past ten years my sister has occupied the entire eighth floor of a grand old apartment building, with gargoyles and sash windows and a rickety elevator that clicks and wheezes like an old furnace. I got off at her floor — her private foyer, actually, empty but for a pair of yellow rain boots — and when I rang the bell, Rachel answered. She was wearing one of her father's dress shirts, with purple high heels and a pink satin conical hat dripping with mylar ribbons.

'Hey Rachel!' I exclaimed, squatting. 'Gimme five, girl!'

'I'm not Rachel,' she replied. 'I'm the Princess of Narnia,' and she suspiciously gathered up her father's shirttails. This was not the greeting I expected. The way we talked every week, I thought I'd get a leap and a hug and a frank request for any presents I might have brought. Instead I stood there waiting while Rachel screwed her index finger deep into her ear.

Finally I asked if I could come in. Warily she stepped aside.

'I like your outfit,' I told her.

'My dad bought me the hat and my mom bought me the high heels but my dad doesn't like me to wear the high heels because he says I'm going to break my leg.'

'High heels are hard,' I agreed.

'My dad's in France, though,' and she cocked her head and smiled conspiratorially, and in that one heart-stopping instant I saw my mother's ghost in her eyes. 'So he'll never know!' she crowed, and with a flourish she hitched up her shirttails and wobbled out of the foyer. 'Mom!' she called down a long dark hall. 'Aunt Izzy's here! Mom! MOM! She's sleeping,' she told me.

'Don't wake her,' I said.

'It's okay, she sleeps a lot,' Rachel said. 'MOM! Are you staying overnight?'

''Til tomorrow,' I said. 'Then I have to go home.'

'You can sleep in my room if you want,' she offered. 'I have a Tigger pillow, you know, and I think I'm getting a Tweety pillow for Christmas — '

She was interrupted by my sister, who had appeared in the doorway and who did look to have been pulled from a deep, drugged sleep. There were little puffed-up sacs under her eyes, and one cheek was reddishly imprinted with fabric folds.

'Hey, Bella,' Ellie said, closing her eyes. 'Give me a hug, my sweet beloved sister.'

She pressed her face against my neck like a

small child and wouldn't let go, as if one of us was putting off bad news. She smelled of turpentine, and I remember thinking she shouldn't be painting in such nice clothes. Lord, I can think the most off-the-wall things at the most meaningful times. To atone for this, I hugged her more tightly, and it became silly, and we laughed.

True to form, my sister looked different; she had cut her hair short and spiky, and pierced a constellation of holes up the side of one ear. As usual she was dressed in black, her bulky sweater leaving only a few inches of skirt showing above her knees. Tights, flats. No jewelry. And she had lost weight again — too much weight, in my view, but I didn't say anything. I don't like to rock any large, personal boats with my sister. Ellie has, over the years, been diagnosed by various doctors as clinically depressed, manic-depressive, borderline, obsessive-compulsive, and phobic to boot. She's been on a variety of medications since college, when she called us in Seattle one night from a Dunkin' Donuts somewhere in upstate New York, threatening to drive her car into a lake. I called the local police, the wrong thing to do, because we didn't hear from her for two weeks, after which we got a phone call from some smooth-voiced woman doctor informing us that Ellie had committed herself to a retreat over in New Hampshire.

'Bad genes,' Ellie will say with a shrug to anyone who asks.

And even at forty, I don't know what to do or say about any of this. It has everything to do with feeling guilty for not falling apart myself over the years, but loving my sister, and wanting to understand how nothing can turn to something, something big and black and bottomless, in the blink of an eye.

That night in New York it was just the three of us, Wilson having left for France a few weeks earlier. Ellie gave me the option of sleeping with Rachel in the extra twin bed, or sleeping with her in their king-size bed in the room overlooking Central Park. I chose the twin bed, and not just because of Rachel's stunned look of betrayal at the very notion of a choice. I chose it because Ellie and I had spent many nights in the same bed after our mother died, and I was afraid that her smells and sounds in the night would hook me up to a battery of feelings that after a quarter of a century I didn't want to feel again.

I took them out to dinner that night, and it would have been fine except Ellie kept talking as though Rachel weren't there. She told me about the new medication she was on and how it gave her headaches and dried out her mouth but thank God, at least she could come again — did I have any idea what it was like to hang on the edge of an orgasm for forty-five minutes? She told me that Rachel was really good at math and really good at art but with reading, *well*. She told me about a father she'd met at Rachel's school, nothing more than a little flirting but it was fun and frankly it put a little more spark into the sex with Wilson, shall we even call it that when you've been doing the same thing day in and day out for ten years?

I wanted to hear about all this, but not with Rachel sitting there.

'So Rachel,' I said. 'What's your favorite subject?'

'Recess,' Rachel said.

'They all say that,' Ellie told me. 'She's really very good at math.'

'How's your teacher?' I asked. 'Do you like her?'

Ellie said, 'It's a he, actually.'

'And he's really cool because he shaves his head,' Rachel said, swinging her legs so fast she knocked the table leg. 'I'm going to shave my head someday.'

'Dream on, kiddo,' Ellie said.

Rachel glared at her. 'Dad said I could.'

'Yes, well, Dad says a lot of things.'

'How's soccer?' I inquired.

'They're making her play goalie,' Ellie said. 'I don't want her to play goalie.'

'I like goalie,' Rachel said. 'You get to dive.'

'She's much better at forward,' Ellie told me.

I wished my sister would just unplug herself for a few moments. It bothered me that she wouldn't let Rachel answer for herself. Also, though it would have been inappropriate, I wanted to ask Rachel just how much her mother was sleeping, and did she ever stay up all night, or lock herself in the bathroom, or pluck out all her eyebrows?

'When's dessert?' Rachel asked.

'Soon,' said Ellie. 'Finish your tortellini.'

'It's got sauce,' Rachel whined.

Ellie sighed, then signaled the waiter and

ordered ice cream for Rachel and another glass of wine for us. While Rachel busied herself with a tiny pitcher of melted chocolate, Ellie fished in her purse for some Nicorette.

'So brief me,' she said. 'What's up with the fertility shit?'

Gabe and I had at that point reached the five-year mark, with medical bills in the low thirties. In fact the year before Ellie had persuaded me to accept a small chunk of money to pay off some of the bills. What else could I do? We were desperate, the bills were coming no longer from the doctor but from a collection agency, and with my practice at a slow point we simply didn't have the money.

And her gift, or this loan, wouldn't have been a big deal, except that I never mentioned it to Gabe. Since I manage our finances, he never noticed, and I told myself it wasn't a lie, just an omission of fact and of course some day I would set things straight.

'Do you need more money?' Ellie was asking.

I shook my head.

'Okay,' and she waited expectantly, and when I didn't elaborate she said, 'so . . . what are you doing about it?'

'Nothing, right now.'

'No more Clomid? No nothing?' She tightened the corners of her mouth in disapproval. 'Time for a little in vitro, maybe?'

'Like we could afford it.'

'Are you deaf? I told you, I'll pay for it.'

'That won't work.'

'Why not?'

'Gabe, for starters. He'd have a fit.'

Ellie flounced back in her chair. 'You let him control your life.'

'I do not. Look, I'm old. My eggs are old. You know what my doctor calls them? Bruised apples at the bottom of the barrel.'

'How poetic.'

'Ellie,' I said, 'I'm forty.'

'That's not old.'

'After five years and no baby, I think it's safe to assume.'

'That's the trouble with you, Izzy,' Ellie said. 'You always just want to sit back and let nature take its course. Ms. Come-What-May.'

Rachel had poured Sweet'N Low onto her ice cream and was now stirring everything into a muddy paste. Suddenly Ellie's face lit up. 'Hey, want my eggs?'

At first I thought it was a joke. But my sister waited so patiently I realized she was serious. 'Ellie,' I said, 'if my eggs are old, then what are yours?'

'Excuse me, but did you forget that I froze a batch? Thirty-five-year-old eggs,' she crooned, as though dangling jewels before my eyes. 'One of which turned into Rachel.'

Rachel looked up.

'That's you, sweetie pie,' Ellie said, tweaking her nose. 'Remember the story of your conception?'

Rachel squinted. 'You mean how I'm a test-tube baby?'

'That's right, honey,' Ellie said. 'Now eat your sundae and let us talk some more. So anyway,' she said to me, 'there's a perfectly good batch of frozen eggs just waiting for you a couple of blocks away.'

I felt like she was recommending some kind of new, cholesterol-free product, now in the freezer section of your local grocery store.

'I don't think so,' I said.

'Is it Gabe? It's Gabe, isn't it? He has something against my eggs, doesn't he?'

'Of course not.'

'So what's the harm in trying?' When I didn't reply, she finished off her wine. 'Way to take the bull by the horns, Isabel. What's wrong with you? God, I'm offering you a good batch of eggs and you won't do anything about it.'

'Frozen eggs don't have much of a success rate, you know. Besides, it would still cost a fortune, and we're not taking any more money from you.'

'Gee, it's nice to know that my previous gift was so well appreciated.'

'I didn't mean it that way.'

Ellie scrutinized my face. 'Did you ever tell Gabe about the money?'

I didn't answer, and she glanced at the ceiling fans. 'I get it. You didn't tell him about the first handout, so now you don't want to complicate things by taking a second handout. Especially when we're talking about eggs, not money, since you'd have to tell him — I mean it'd be pretty hard to keep a batch of eggs secret, wouldn't it? And then who knows what might come out?'

I looked around for the waiter, thinking Ellie was getting way too pushy. At times like this, you have to rewrite the script.

'To tell you the truth,' I said, 'we're thinking maybe we don't even want children.'

'Ha ha,' said Ellie. 'Very funny.'

'Well, we're not going to do in vitro. Not with my eggs, not with yours.'

Rachel looked up from her sundae. 'Where do eggs come from?'

'From your ovaries,' Ellie answered loudly, capturing the attention of the couple at the next table. Ellie glared back, and they quickly bowed their heads.

'Guess I'll just have to use them myself,' she sighed.

'You mean have another baby?' Rachel shrieked.

'Maybe,' Ellie said.

'You're forty-two,' I reminded her.

'That's why I froze my eggs,' she pointed out. 'Just in case I changed my mind. And if Wilson doesn't want to spend the money, that's too bad. I mean, it's my money too, isn't it? Don't I contribute to the household? Just because I don't work outside the home doesn't mean I'm not entitled to the money he brings home.'

How did we get onto the subject of Ellie's lack of a steady income? Why on earth would it matter, given what Wilson makes? Was my sister really thinking of having another child? Or was she saying this out of spite, because I'd refused her eggs?

'Look, Ellie,' I said, 'I'm tired, and you are too. Let's get the check. Rachel? Are you finished?'

Rachel pushed her bowl away; I could hear my

father clucking at the waste. I managed to catch the waiter's eye and signaled for the check. Our dinner was over, our conversation had lost focus, and it was time to go. Several times during the long wait Ellie started to say something, but mostly she stared at the salt shaker. Finally the waiter brought the check, and as I laid out my credit card, Ellie started jiggling her foot.

'Listen to me, going on and on,' she said dully. 'Here's the question. Why is it, when I'm the one with the healthy child and two houses and all the money I'll ever need, when I'm the one who gets this great gallery to show my work, when all my friends get breast cancer and I've never had even one goddamn abnormal Pap — why is it that out of all these other people, you included, I'm the one who needs the meds?'

'Don't hate me,' I begged.

'I don't.' She drew deeply on an imaginary cigarette and blew smoke rings. 'It's her I hate.'

Rachel looked up. 'Who? Who do you hate?'

4

As children we grew up in the Leschi neighborhood of Seattle. Our house was nothing fancy, a bungalow of shakes built forty-nine steps up from the street against a hillside of twisted madrona trees. My parents bought the house right after Ellie was born, having argued for weeks over it — my mother liking its isolation way up there on the hillside, my father, a personal injury lawyer, worrying about the forty-nine steps. He had wanted to buy a house over in Mount Baker, a sun-drenched Seattle box with a picket fence and a soft green lawn and rhododendrons flanking the front porch. I knew what it looked like because once when Ellie and I complained about living high up on the side of a hill, my mother drove us by the box and told us we ought to be more grateful for what we had. Frankly I would have preferred the neighborhood of boxes; there were kids playing on the lawns and riding their bikes on the sidewalk, and I might have had a friend next door.

But my mother had great plans for our house. It had a sunny yellow kitchen with a window above the sink overlooking a lumpy little backyard lawn. Across the yard, facing a rutted back alleyway, stood a dilapidated single-car garage. The living room had a stone fireplace, and the floors had settled with a quaint slant.

Upstairs there were two bedrooms: a larger one for my parents, and a smaller one for Ellie and me. Our room had slanted ceilings and gaudy roses blooming on pale green wallpaper and an ornate heating grate that looked directly down into the kitchen. Through the dormer window, if the weather was clear, you could see Mount Rainier.

When Ellie and I were very young, my mother terraced in a garden on the steep slope of our front yard, using old railroad ties and cyclone fencing. This she did while my father was down in Portland on some case, all by herself, to surprise him. Apparently she put us both in a playpen on the porch and gave us a bowl of M&Ms to keep us happy — a memory she would later relate with great pride, as though we would admire such motherly attendance to our wants and needs. We were way beyond playpen age, I was maybe two and Ellie four. The bottom must have bowed under our weight, and I'm sure we could easily have climbed over the railing. But we never questioned our mother's decision. For all we knew, every pair of sisters got plunked into a playpen with a bowl of candy while their mother went out to garden.

While Ellie and I sat and ate our M&Ms, our mother lugged and hoisted and dug and hoed the hill into a passable garden. There was little sun because of all the madrona trees, so she couldn't plant the flowers she had grown up with back East, the zinnias and pansies and hollyhocks that lined the walkways of Nana's house in New Hampshire. Instead she planted the shady perennials — camellia and bleeding heart and primrose — and hoped for the best. They did not fare well. Year after year she dug them up and set out new varieties, and usually by July the garden was grown over with a loose-rooted weed with a lacy network of leaves and small pink flowers. It was a pretty weed, actually, but my mother would make Ellie and me tear it up by the handful, stuffing it into paper bags which would reek with its limy perfume as we carried it all back to the trash.

One year when Nana came to visit, she brought a hundred daffodil bulbs. She and my mother put on these old flowered pedal pushers that made their hips look too wide and got out there on their hands and knees, digging and measuring and digging some more, until our unhappy terraced garden was pockmarked with holes. Then Ellie and I — older and no longer confined to the playpen — got to go along with a sack of bone meal, sprinkling a tablespoon into each hole, after which my mother would set in one of the misshapen brown bulbs, carefully making sure its wormy dried-up roots faced down, its papery tip up. Nana would follow, filling in the hole and packing it down. When the hundred bulbs were all in place, Nana took us out to the A&W. She said anyone could grow daffodils, anywhere. I was full of hope.

The daffodils were the one thing that worked in our garden. Next spring, right around Easter, our hillside burst into color with yellow trumpets everywhere. It was a spectacle that brought our unseen neighbors climbing the forty-nine steps with their cameras, and even a photographer from the newspaper came to memorialize the moment. His black-and-white photo of our garden made the front page, but I was disappointed; it was a smudgy and colorless reproduction of one of the most wondrous sights I at that age had ever seen.

After that my mother was on a roll. For some reason her luck changed and our blanched perennials, which for several years had begrudged us one or two blooms at most, blossomed with a competitive frenzy into splashes of exotic color. There were enough flowers for bouquets in every room, including the bathroom. Nana thought it was the bone meal. My mother insisted it was because she talked to the plants. Ellie said it was because we'd had so much rain that winter.

I myself didn't buy any of their ideas. To me, it was an act of God, plain and simple. Beauty had come to our house. We were in luck.

★ ★ ★

Nana came to visit often. She was afraid of airplanes, so she took a bus from Manchester, New Hampshire, to Montreal, then a train across Canada to Vancouver, and finally a bus down to Seattle. She never came without presents. Always there were new clothes, and not just a skirt or a top but a whole outfit, with the tights and the belt and the little purse to match. Usually these outfits were identical in design but of different colors. Long ago Nana had decided that I looked good in pink and Ellie in blue. I hated pink, but always thanked Nana. I knew about manners.

She usually brought a few toys, too, and books, and something for the house, and something very expensive and luxurious for my mother. One year it was a set of silk pajamas, orange Chinese pedal-pusher things with embroidered buttons and a Nehru collar. My mother also knew about manners, and she thanked Nana, but she put them in a drawer and never wore them.

Nana had a good heart. She was a small, tidy woman with gray hair, which she always wore in a tight bun that clung to the nape of her neck like a little mouse. She wore woolen suits and nylon stockings and low-heeled loafers. Her luggage matched, and there was always one of those round hatboxes that held some feather-daubed thing with a veil. It was for church. We never went to church, but whenever Nana came to visit, my mother would remind us not to make plans for Sunday morning. She needn't have worried. I looked forward to these religious excursions, especially if one of them coincided with the Easter service, with its white lilies and hallelujah choruses.

'Your Reverend has a great deal of insight,' Nana would remark later, over the ham and scalloped potato dinner she'd prepared. Nana liked to cook, especially for our family, all of whom she saw as so thin and in need of nourishment. I ate gigantic portions of whatever she made, which only served to confirm my grandmother's view that our family was out here on the West Coast starving to death.

'Aren't you lucky to have a man like him,' she went on. 'Didn't he give a beautiful sermon?'

'What's a sermon?' I asked.

Nana smiled broadly. 'Pardon me?'

'It was a lovely sermon,' my mother interjected. 'But he's a busy man. I don't see very much of him.'

'Oh, but you ought to,' Nana said. 'A good minister is always there when you need a shoulder to cry on.'

'I don't need a shoulder to cry on,' my mother said. 'I've got Hugh.'

'When Hugh isn't enough,' Nana said.

Nana's visits also meant a trip to Antoine's on a late Sunday afternoon. Antoine's was the only restaurant in Seattle that Nana liked. It was a dreary, windowless place with white tablecloths and red leather chairs, too much silverware and always a bouquet of funereal white mums in the entryway. As children Ellie and I learned quickly to avoid anything with the word *rognons* in it, because that meant some dangerous kind of organ meat. Our safest bet was the *canard à l'orange*, which came with a towering pile of *pommes frites* and a sauce that tasted like marmalade. My father ordered the *steak au poivre*, but my mother invariably found some reason to go on a food strike at Antoine's, and she would order a cup of lobster bisque, to be polite, but would not touch it. Nana herself ordered the complicated-sounding specialties, and dessert was a happy affair for all of us, because they made *crêpes flambées* right there at the table, and with *l'addition* came a plate of chocolate truffles.

Antoine's looms in my memory because Ellie got her first period there. I was nine and she was eleven, and my mother had been on this salmon kick for a month, so that when Nana came to visit she found us thin and pale and badly in need of a good piece of red meat. Time for Antoine's, she decided, and it was during this meal that my sister grew up, and grew away from me, in a way I found unbearable at the time.

We were waiting for the main course when Ellie got up to use the restroom, and as she walked away we all noticed the telltale blot on the back of her skirt. 'Whoops,' my mother said, as casually as if Ellie'd just burped. Nana bit her lip. My father, always Mister Calm, sat there taking in the whole scene with a bemused look on his face. I couldn't look at him. Fathers weren't supposed to be around at moments like this.

My mother excused herself, and hurried after Ellie, which left Nana, me, and my father at the table. I thought I was going to die. My mother had told Ellie and me about periods, but I had no idea it would happen just like that, with no warning. I thought you would at least have a little say over the matter so you wouldn't end up with a blot on the back of your skirt in a fancy restaurant.

After a long time my mother came back and sat down and said that Ellie had locked herself in a stall and wouldn't come out. Nana reminded my mother that dinner was about to be served, but my mother only shrugged, and said that if Ellie wanted to stay in the bathroom until it was time to go, that was fine with her. Then she launched into a long, breezy story about the first time she got her period, how the blood was brown and not red, and how she didn't have a clue about sanitary napkins since Nana'd never mentioned them, come to think of it Nana never mentioned anything about the male or female reproductive systems the entire time my mother was growing up, now did she?

I didn't eat a thing.

Ellie never did return to the table. When we'd finished and Nana was paying the bill, my mother took Ellie's coat into the ladies' room, and a minute later Ellie marched out past the front desk, through the frosted glass door, and out into the afternoon mist.

'She could at least say thank you,' Nana remarked.

That was the first time I couldn't talk to my sister. She had crossed over into a new world, and I wanted to know what it was like, but I felt too shy to ask and she didn't volunteer anything. Over the next few days she spent an inordinate amount of time in the bathroom. We went through rolls of toilet paper, and Ellie was always emptying the wastebaskets, but still she didn't volunteer anything and I didn't have the courage to ask. At one point I heard my grandmother scold her for using too many napkins, and Ellie called her a bitch right to her face, and my father stepped in and sent Ellie out to sweep the forty-nine steps.

And one day it was over, because Ellie began wearing nighties again instead of pajamas, and stopped emptying the wastebasket, and she began to talk to me again.

I think Ellie getting her period triggered something between my mother and Nana, because Nana left a few days later, and after her departure my mother went on one of her cleaning and exterminating binges, which she always did when she was upset over something. New rubber gloves, new mops, powders and bleaches and gallons of some homemade window cleaner. She sprayed the base-boards for black widows. She vacuumed the rafters of the attic and basement. She carried boxes out to the garage. She called Roto Rooter to scrub out the pipes. She put this blue stuff into the toilet, which turned green when we peed. She sent Ellie and me to school with these plastic toilet-seat liners, so we wouldn't get hepatitis. And at night she went to sleep wearing lotion-filled gloves, because her hands were so chapped from all the scrubbing.

And then it was daffodil time again. They were more beautiful than ever because they had spread down the hill, almost to the road. People took pictures. We had daffodils in the kitchen, the bedrooms, the bathroom. I tried to press one in a book, but the results were disappointing. The trumpet shape was lost, and the pure yellow color leached into the pages of the book. It was not worth trying to preserve that kind of beauty.

5

The first time Gabe and I officially went out, it was to another Antoine's, in San Francisco. We were just getting to know each other, and I thought it would amuse him to hear about the Seattle Antoine's, about the piles of *pommes frites*, and Nana ordering the most complicated dishes, and my father wedging an olive onto one of his front teeth and sneaking a smile at Ellie and me. I didn't tell him about my mother's food strikes, though, or about Ellie hiding out in the bathroom with a blot on her skirt. I told him only the good things about my family, because I had an inkling things were going to go somewhere with this man, and I didn't want to scare him off.

As a result, when he asked if my parents still ate at the Seattle Antoine's, I had to correct him. I told him the usual story. Car crash. Instant death. He bought it all, which made me want to cry.

★ ★ ★

'Happy birthday,' says Gabe.

Sunlight leaks across our bed on this warm Saturday morning. Gabe moves close and drapes his thigh over my hip. Even though we've been having a lot of sex since he moved back, whenever we begin anything, my blood pressure

46

rises a few points. When you've spent the last six years fucking with a purpose, it's pretty much impossible to fuck for the fun of it at the drop of a hat.

What's been relatively easy is sharing the same bed again. We know our places, we know who gets which pillow and when to cuddle and when to roll over and leave the other person alone. The sheets have that smell of coupling again, of warm breath and dampness, a mussed-up doggy smell. When I sleep alone, I am as tidy as an ant. Together, we tangle everything within reach.

'What time is it?'

'I don't know. Do you like that?' he whispers.

I like it a lot.

'How about that?'

I turn to face him. He runs his hands down my back, around to the inside hollow between my thighs. With the sun upon us both, he kicks the rumpled sheet off the foot of the bed and I find myself making just one simple wish: to forget about biology, and lose myself with him once again.

★　★　★

Gabe is in the shower when the phone rings, and I answer it, expecting some friend who has gone through a datebook and remembered my birthday. But it's Wilma, who bluntly informs me that her daughter just got some lab results back.

'Tracy's got cancer,' she says flatly.

I sit down on the edge of the bed. I didn't

know Tracy was being tested for anything. 'Are you sure?'

Wilma says yes, they are quite sure. They biopsied a mole last week, she says. She didn't tell me because . . . well, she doesn't know why she didn't tell me. She should have. She's sorry.

It grieves me that at a time like this, Wilma is worrying about my feeling left out. 'What's her prognosis?'

Fifty-fifty, Wilma tells me.

'That's good,' I say, 'isn't it?'

Wilma guesses that it depends on which way you flip the coin, and I feel stupid.

Wilma clears her throat, and I sense that she is coming to the real point of the phone call.

'Isabel,' she says, 'in view of all this, we're going to drop the custody case. See, Tracy has to have radiation and chemo, so she and Erin are going to come live with us for a while. That way Carl and I can take care of Erin while Tracy goes for the treatments. And since we're not fighting over Erin, we don't need a lawyer. Plus of course we need to save our money.'

'Of course.'

'But I wanted you to know,' she goes on, 'well, I don't like lawyers and I never wanted to have to go to a lawyer in the first place, but I'm really glad,' she says, 'I'm really glad that I know you.'

Call waiting beeps.

'Carl feels the same,' Wilma goes on. 'He said to me last night, you gotta hand it to her, the gal's never tried to drive in the wedge. And he's right. There's no enemy here. There's no other side. I don't think too many lawyers would have seen that. You're a good soul, hon.' She is silent for a while, and then I hear her say, in a muffled voice, 'I'll be off in a minute. You go get your ba-ba. Well, anyway,' she says to me, 'we've got a tough row to hoe but sometimes it's things like this that pull a family back together again. Silver linings, I guess you'd say.'

I ask how Erin is doing.

Wilma laughs wearily. 'Oh, Erin's happy as a clam. She moved right into her room and there are neighborhood kids for her to play with, not like that apartment in the middle of Denver. And Tracy can see this. She loves that little girl. Sometimes I think Erin's the only thing that keeps Tracy going, with all that crazy worrying she does about poisoning everyone.'

Call waiting beeps again.

'Well anyway, send me the bill,' Wilma says. 'And I'll keep in touch. I'll let you know how things are going. How's everything with you, by the way?'

'Oh, fine,' I say. 'My family's coming out this weekend.'

'Well, you hug them and tell them you love them,' Wilma says. 'You bury any old hatchets you've got lying around, you hear? I mean that. Life's too short. Goodbye, honey.'

By this time, the other caller has hung up. I stare at my feet, thinking more about mothers and daughters than about Tracy's melanoma. Is that how it works? Your kids keep you from killing yourself when you think you can't take it anymore?

It didn't stop my mother.

49

Gabe appears in the doorway, toweling off. He pats his head gently, to avoid further hair loss. 'Who was that?' he asks, dropping his towel on the floor.

'A client,' I say. 'Former client, now.' And I tell him about Wilma and Carl and the custody case that is no more.

'Melanoma,' Gabe says. 'Shit. I had a friend who had melanoma.'

'Did he live?'

'No.'

'Then don't tell me any more,' I say. 'Have you seen my biking shorts?'

'Aren't we going on a hike?'

Wilma's phone call has unsettled me, for reasons I can't yet articulate. 'It's too hot.'

'Not too hot to bike, though?'

I don't answer. Gabe wads up his towel and places it on the bed, where he thinks it will dry.

'Okay,' he says. 'It's your birthday, you call the shots.'

I search for the sarcasm in his voice, but find none. He truly means it. I feel ashamed. He is a good man, just trying to give me what I need today.

Before I can figure out how to be gracious, the phone rings again. 'I'm not here,' I tell him, but he has already answered it and is saying Yes, hold on, and then he hands it to me.

'Don't you have call waiting?' Ellie demands.

'I was with a client. What do you want?'

'Hey toots, don't bitch at me when I'm coming out to celebrate your birthday.'

'Where are you?'

'Over New Jersey. We just left. We wanted to say happy birthday. Here's Rachel.' I hear muffled voices, sounds of distress, and then Ellie comes back on. 'Well, I thought it would make her feel better but I guess not.'

'Is everything all right?'

'Who knows, with this child,' Ellie says wearily.

'What do you mean?'

'Nothing, though God, I just got her calmed down and now she's crying again.'

'Calmed down from what?'

'Oh, I'll tell you later. Shit happens, you know? Happy birthday, Isabella. What are you doing, anyway?'

'Going on a bike ride.'

'So go, I'm not keeping you,' sniffs Ellie.

'I didn't say you were!'

'I can hear it in your voice. 'How the fuck long is she gonna take?' '

'What time are you getting in?'

'We'll get there when we get there,' Ellie says. 'Happy ride. She's too busy to talk,' I hear her say to Rachel, right before hanging up.

I hang up, annoyed. Why did she call? Just to say happy birthday, when she's going to be out here in a few hours? Nothing makes sense right now. I go downstairs to the garage, where it is about three hundred degrees Fahrenheit. I hoist my bicycle down from its hooks and pull a shoulder muscle. My derailleur is jammed, and in tugging at the dirt-caked chain I manage to break a nail and lodge a speck of dust the size of a fucking rock in my eye.

51

You doing okay, Izzy? my father asks, from miles away.

I'm doing okay, Dad.

You'll rally. You always manage to rally. I'm proud of you, Izzy. Your mother would be proud of you, too.

And if I was just managing to hang on, his reference to my mother taps a crack in the eggshell. She would be sixty-nine now, and with my father's words I imagine her driving a convertible, wearing rhinestone-studded sunglasses and a bright red scarf around her head. Chain-smoking, throwing her cigarette butts out the window. Dark lipstick and long nails and freckled arms, loose skin under her chin and a pacemaker under her breast and a tiny, shivering Yorkshire terrier in her lap. She is coming to visit me, with the back seat full of brightly wrapped packages and flowers and a bottle of champagne and a three-layer chocolate cake in a white box tied with string. Nobody does birthdays like your mother.

I straddle my bike, downshift, and pedal hard up the hill. At the top, there is a large flat rock by the side of the road. Often I have seen a red fox sitting on that rock, quietly switching his white-tipped tail as he gazes out over the Great Plains. Though I am only half a mile from home, I coast to a stop, drop my bike in the gravel, and take my place upon the fox's rock. I am violating the rules, but on your birthday you can do whatever you want, even piss off a fox, if it helps you get through.

6

When I was five, my mother went off to a hospital for a month. My father couldn't afford a housekeeper, so Nana came out to help. She took good care of us. She cooked a lot of meat, and darned my father's socks, and took us shopping for new underwear and the stiff white petticoats Ellie and I both coveted. Every morning she woke us by seven so there'd be time for a good breakfast, time for braids and ribbons and socks that matched. She was there when we got home after school. Dinner was always at five-thirty, bath time at seven, and every night we got tucked beneath our woolly green blankets by eight.

That was when we missed our mother the most. To settle us for bed Nana told us stories about our mother's childhood — how she fell through the ice, or got lost at the beach. These stories all contained elements of danger, a mild danger from which my mother always escaped. They made Ellie and me feel safe, because they served as a parable for our present situation. Our mother had been in another kind of danger, right? And she went away, but soon she would come home, and everything would be okay, right?

Nothing could feel very safe for very long, though, not when your mother was off in a special hospital and nobody would say what exactly was wrong. And Nana's home-cooked meals and stories were no substitute for having our mother with us, in the flesh. Every night, as we lay across from each other in our twin beds, I asked Ellie when our mother was coming home. Ellie, who seemed to know so much more than I did, always promised that she'd be home by Friday. Or Monday. Or Saturday. And never once, even after she was proven wrong time and time again, did I doubt her.

The day did come when our mother came home, and I remember it feeling like Christmas, as though I was about to be given a very big and important present. That morning, while my father was picking her up at the hospital, Ellie and I passed the time in the kitchen with Nana, coloring pictures while Nana baked bread.

At some point the Plymouth quietly rolled to a stop in front of the garage. Ellie and I scrambled to the window and watched as our father got out, solemnly waved to us, and went around to open my mother's door. But she had already opened it herself. I saw her rising, turning to the kitchen door, searching, locating me and Ellie in the lower half of the window and placing both hands against her cheeks and closing her eyes. She wore a blue silk scarf tied around her head, peasant-style, and I worried that she might be bald. We'd been told so little about her hospital stay that I'd come up with my own theories, many of which included some kind of dramatic disfigurement.

My mother rushed up the muddy walkway and Ellie and I flew out the door and into her arms. Inside, Nana bustled about, brewing tea and slicing bread; and my mother brought out presents, which further confirmed my Christmas theory. She had a green ceramic leprechaun for Ellie and a pink musical merry-go-round for me, with little ducks that bobbed and pecked as they spun around. We gave her our drawings. Nobody could stop hugging.

But eventually, Ellie couldn't resist playing with my merry-go-round, which infuriated me, so I took her leprechaun, whereupon she pushed me against the stove, which singed the tips of my braids. Nana scolded Ellie and made us both surrender our gifts. My father told Nana that wasn't fair and made her give back the gifts, while he went about opening up the windows to air out the smell of burnt hair. My mother simply left the room.

That evening we all ate Nana's ham dinner in the dining room, with candles and a tablecloth, and Ellie and I got seconds of dessert. Afterward, our mother gave us our baths, but I felt shy with her, and could not kiss her goodnight.

★ ★ ★

Your mother needed a rest, was all Nana ever said. I didn't understand why she couldn't have rested at home. She had a nice bed, a room to herself, dark green shades to shut out the light. What more could she need?

★ ★ ★

With my mother home, life was perfect. Nana went back to New Hampshire, and I was glad to see her go. My mother let us have Trix for breakfast instead of gluey oatmeal, and we got Franco-American for lunch, and TV dinners in their partitioned aluminum trays, even though we didn't have a TV. In the evening we piled into our parents' bed and our mother read to us until we fell asleep. Sometimes she persuaded our father to let us sleep there for the night, and he would go off and sleep in one of our beds. And if we woke up late the next morning, our mother drove us to school and lied to the teachers about heavy traffic. Nobody else in my class was so lucky.

That year my kindergarten class put on a play about the first Thanksgiving, for which we made Pilgrim hats out of construction paper. Both my parents were in the audience, my father having come straight from work in a tidy dark suit and tie and a white shirt. My mother sat beside him. Ever since she'd come home from the hospital, she'd been wearing the blue silk scarf around her head, and today was no different, except that she'd wrapped it tightly, turban-style, so you could not see any hair whatsoever. All the other mothers wore crisp shirtwaists and high heels, but my mother wore turquoise pedal pushers and an old white shirt of my father's, with dull black rubbers stretched tightly over her saddle shoes.

Yet nothing about my mother's appearance struck me as strange, not at that age. She was my mother, and she was here, not off in some hospital being treated for something I did not know about. After I successfully carried the bowl of corn across the stage, she stood up and applauded. She was the only parent to do so, and while many children might have wanted to shrink from embarrassment, I merely bowed my head, unable to disguise a complicit smile. I had done well. She was proud of me.

Afterward there was a little party, with popcorn and cranberry juice. Parents stood about, chatting. As I folded my paper hat to take home with me, I overheard my mother telling a group she had cancer, which was why she was wearing the scarf. That was the first time I'd heard the word, and it seemed as good an explanation as any.

Not for Ellie. 'Cancer?' she shrieked that night as I burrowed beneath my covers. 'She doesn't have cancer! You die from cancer! She's not dying!'

'That's what she told Mrs. Crane.'

'Well, she's lying.'

'No she isn't.'

'Yes she is.'

'No she isn't!' I shouted, and in another moment the hall light flicked on and my father's broad-shouldered form appeared in the doorway.

'Stop fighting,' he said. 'What are you fighting about?'

Ellie told him what I had said.

'Izzie?' my father said, sitting on the edge of my bed. 'Is that what you think?'

I picked at the paint chipping off the rungs of my bed. 'That's what she told Mrs. Crane.'

'Well,' and my father took my hands in his, to keep me from picking at the paint, 'maybe you heard her wrong.'

'I didn't hear her wrong.'

'Maybe she misspoke. But she doesn't have cancer. She's not sick.'

'Told you,' Ellie said.

In the end I gave in and admitted that I was mistaken, but inside I clung to the notion that my mother had spoken the truth, that she did in fact have this nameable disease. It was better than nothing.

★   ★   ★

With so many TV dinners it was only a matter of time before we bought our first television set. For this major event, we all drove downtown to a department store and took the escalator up to the fourth floor, where there were rows and rows of great bulky consoles, all flickering in black and white on the same station. Ellie and I hopped back and forth from one console to another, pressing our noses to the gray blur, playing with the rabbit ears on top to fuzz and unfuzz the picture.

My parents were at the far end, examining the budget-priced models perched on wobbly iron racks. My mother stood back and watched while my father changed the channels and fiddled with the antennae. My mother shook her head. My father went to another model and did the same thing, and my mother shook her head again. It was too grainy, she said. Not enough contrast.

Too small a screen. My father began to lose patience, and told her that if she wanted a better picture they were going to have to spend more money, and they didn't have more money, and if she wanted any television at all it would have to be one of these, even if the picture was a little grainy. My mother said she had a headache, pulled a pack of Winstons from her pocket, and went and sat down in a Barcalounger for a smoke.

Eventually my father picked out the television, and we took it home that day. Since we'd already gotten the antenna installed, we could hook it up immediately, and as soon as we turned it on, our lives changed. What a miracle it was! Right here in our living room, a little girl with ringlets sang and tap-danced across the stage. Ellie and I couldn't move. It seemed impossible that any child could dance that well. We watched her twirl and stomp and click her heels and finally, when she was done, she gave a clap and opened her arms wide, balancing on one foot.

'Why, that's Shirley Temple,' my mother said. 'I used to watch her in the movie theaters when I was a little girl.'

'I want to be like her,' Ellie said.

'I do, too,' I said.

'You can't,' Ellie informed me. 'I wanted to first.'

'You both can,' my mother said. 'Who wants to take dance lessons?'

'I do!' I said.

'I don't if she does,' Ellie said.

'Oh, don't be such a sourpuss,' my mother

59

said to Ellie. 'You both can take dance lessons. Wouldn't that be so cute, Hugh?' she said to our father. 'We could curl their hair and dress them up and they could go on Amateur Hour!'

'Well, let's not jump the gun,' my father said. 'If the girls want to take dance lessons, fine. Amateur Hour, I'd say let's wait on that.'

Two days later my mother enrolled us both in dance lessons. Our teacher's name was Nance, not Nans-see, she pointed out, just plain Nance, rhymes with dance. She wore a long golden scarf wrapped around her neck, black leotard, black skirt, and black ballet slippers. There were five other girls in the class, all wearing their hair in ringlets, all dressed in flouncy pink tutus.

'You'll be better than all of them,' our mother whispered to us — words we needed to hear, dressed as we were in corduroy overalls and striped shirts from JC Penney's, our hair hanging bone-straight and cut crooked and choppy above our shoulders. And indeed, I believed my mother. My shoulders felt light, my legs felt as nimble as a marionette's — I could hardly keep them from tapping out the rhythm to some private beat I kept hearing in my head.

Classes met once a week. Tutus were fine, but all mothers had to remain outside in the hallway. Nance put on records and had us lumber like elephants, hop like rabbits, and skip to Irish jigs — nothing that ever remotely resembled ballet or tap or any kind of dance for that matter. At the end of class we gathered for circle time.

And every time I looked at the door, there was the pale sliver of my mother's face, watching

60

through the window.

There was one girl in the class whom Ellie and I could not stand. Her name was Charlene and she was short and bossy and always critical. My elephant was too hoppy, she said, my rabbit too jerky. She told me I would never be able to dance like Shirley Temple. I listened to all of this for a few weeks, until one day I kicked her in the shin.

Charlene fell on the floor, shrieking and rolling and clutching her leg. Nance stopped the record. I knew I was going to get punished, but never at that young age had I felt so richly satisfied. Charlene accused me right away, and without inquiry Nance made me sit on the sidelines, which did not please my mother, who immediately stuck her blue-kerchiefed head inside the door.

'Is something wrong?' she asked with a bright smile.

I knew that smile. It was the smile she used with bigger kids on the playground, the smile she gave my teacher when the teacher informed her I never followed directions. It was a smile of war.

When Nance explained what had happened, my mother remarked, 'Well, she must have deserved it.'

'Well, we don't kick in my class,' Nance said. 'Would you please wait outside?'

My mother returned to her vigil in the hall, and I watched the other children pretend to be ostriches. It was a silly exercise, and Ellie soon dropped out. Coming over to join me, she sat down on the floor and wiggled about to get comfortable. Then she frowned, reached behind her, and picked up a shiny brass thumbtack. We looked at the tack, glanced up at the bulletin board on the wall above us, and looked at Charlene.

Suddenly full of energy, Ellie rejoined the group. Soon it was circle time. When Charlene stopped, Ellie squatted by her side, and nobody actually saw Ellie's hand dart out but no sooner had Charlene sat down than she hopped right back up, yowling and shrieking, twisting around and tugging at her pink tutu until the tack fell like a sparkle of light onto the carpet. Ellie picked it up and gravely held it out for Nance to see.

That was the end of circle time.

'I'm so sorry,' Nance kept saying after class as Charlene, now dark and silent, pressed against her mother's hips. 'You're absolutely right, there should never be thumbtacks in a dance studio. I'm so, so sorry.'

As I was tying my shoes, I saw my mother wink at Ellie. She knew! I reveled in this conspiratorial link. It was one of the few times that my sister, my mother, and I were all on the same side. It made me feel both protected and protective, and a warm feeling spread throughout my limbs. This, I thought, this was what families were all about.

As we were about to leave the studio, with her own mother out of earshot, Charlene approached my mother. 'You should take that scarf off,' she told her. 'Why do you wear it all the time, anyway?'

'Oh, honey, I have tuberculosis,' my mother said.

Charlene backed away.

'A very bad disease,' my mother said. 'You don't want to get it. It makes you cough up blood and your hair falls out and you start menstruating seven days a week. Even very little girls,' she said knowingly.

'I don't believe you,' Charlene said.

'That's your choice, honey,' my mother said. 'Just be sure to wash your hands when you get home.'

Tuberculomas? It sounded like a musical instrument. That night, after an afternoon spent wondering, worrying, reassuring myself and then worrying some more, I asked Ellie about this new disease. Ellie told me what I suspected.

I was quiet for a long time, hugging the covers around me. The window between our bed was open, and the curtains wafted out just enough to keep me from seeing my sister's profile.

'Ellie,' I finally said, 'why does she lie?'

Ellie considered this for a moment.

'She likes her stories better than the truth, I guess,' she finally said.

'So they're stories,' I said. 'Not lies.'

'That's right,' said Ellie.

After that I didn't use the word lie again. I began to think of my mother as a storyteller, like the woman who once came to a friend's birthday party and sat us in a circle and told us fables and tales and . . . well, stories. When my mother told Nana not to come visit one year because she had to photograph the mayor, it was a story. When she told our father she'd taken only one shower that day and the reason her hands were so chapped was from gardening — that too was a story. But when she told Ellie and me that the man she saw every Tuesday and Saturday was not really a doctor but more like a friend — well, that was harder to see as a story. I recognized the name from when she was in the hospital. She was still sick, with something.

But I would not use the word liar.

★   ★   ★

The strange thing is, Ellie remembers very little about dance class, or thumbtacks, or my mother's trip to the hospital. Which is not to say that she has a bad memory. She remembers her second grade teacher down to the color of her nail polish. She remembers the blackberry brambles on our way to school, the red rubbers we stretched over our shoes, the chain letter she broke. She remembers how her best friend's mother got in a car crash that year, and how our mother brought the woman a box of Twinkies in the hospital. She even remembers my white Pilgrim paper hat, how I tacked it up on the wall over my bed as a reminder of my stunning performance.

But she doesn't remember our mother going away, doesn't remember the little green leprechaun or the pink merry-go-round with the bobbing ducks. She doesn't remember the blue silk scarf. She thinks sometimes she remembers our mother dancing in the rain late at night; but even that, she says, might be just a figment of our imagination.

7

It was not our imagination. Our mother did go dancing in the rain. Not often, and never during the day, but there would be a certain kind of rainstorm, the hard, warm, drenching kind, that caught her in the middle of a television show, say, and she would throw open the door to the wind, to the mulchy smell of grass and mud and rotting leaves. 'Oh, girls, it's that smell again!' and she would kick off her shoes and run out into the pouring rain to the back alley, where she would skip through the puddles, arms flung furiously to the drunken sky. Infected, Ellie and I would go running after her, leaping about, splashing in the rutted little finger lakes, opening our mouths to catch the largest raindrop ever to fall upon this earth.

'Oh Hugh, come on out, you big stiff!' my mother would shout, but my father would just smile from the kitchen doorway, a towel over his shoulder. 'You big priss!' she would shout, and she would kick a stream of muddy water toward him. 'What's wrong with you anyway!' Then off she would go, waltzing past sheds and clotheslines and blackberry brambles, shouting strange things into the night, like 'Ai-Yai!' or 'Whoo-hoo!'

Then, just as suddenly as it all began, it would end. My mother would stop in mid-kick, and gaze about, fingering loose tendrils of hair, searching for something that was there just a minute ago. 'Come on in, Mimi,' my father would say gently, having appeared from nowhere with an umbrella, and he would try to take her hand, but she would snatch it away and simply follow him into the house, where she would collapse onto the sofa and light a cigarette. If the television was off she would turn it back on and stare at whatever snowy picture filled the screen. Ellie and I could have turned cartwheels on the living room rug and she wouldn't have noticed.

Once Ellie and I awoke in the pre-dawn January light to snow flurries. We'd never seen it snow in Seattle before, and we raced downstairs and ran outside in our nighties, barefoot, screeching, throwing handfuls of slush at one another. My mother appeared in the doorway in my father's red plaid bathrobe, smoking. She watched us calmly for a few minutes, then threw her cigarette into the snow and ran out to join us, and we all linked arms and she got us kicking up our legs in unison, like the Rockettes.

But then some mishap took place. Maybe I accidentally kicked Ellie, or she hit me, but we began to squabble. It escalated, as squabbles do, and I remember my mother telling us to stop it, but we didn't, and then all of us were shouting, and suddenly my mother grabbed us by the scruff of our necks, like kittens or puppies, and yanked our heads together face to face and screamed, 'You girls fight so, you are going to send me back to the nuthouse!'

It was the first time I'd ever heard that word, but I knew what it meant. I stood frozen in

66

place, staring at my mother. Ellie crossed her arms and gazed off toward the lake. I wanted to tell my mother I was sorry, but I couldn't say anything.

'You fight so goddamn much,' my mother said hoarsely. Then she sighed, and shook her head.

'Oh, everything is so complicated,' she said. 'I shouldn't have said that. That was a bad thing to say. It's not you girls. Will you forget I said that?'

I told her I would.

'Promise?'

I nodded, but Ellie still wouldn't even look at her.

'Come on,' my mother said, holding out her elbows. 'Let's do that dance again.'

Ellie stood there with her arms crossed, and I hung back. The moment was over. I was frightened of my mother, of that terrible voice I'd heard.

'All right,' my mother said dully. 'Come on inside. It's cold — good lord, you're barefoot, your father's going to kill me.' She lit a cigarette and nudged us toward the house.

'I hate the snow,' she said.

★ ★ ★

As I sit here on the fox's rock, looking out over the Great Plains, I'm remembering that scene. I think it was right afterward that Ellie began plucking out her hair on one side of her head, plucked it so much that my mother finally shaved that one whole side, just to make her stop. In response, Ellie started plucking out the

67

other side, and my mother shaved that side too, which made her look like a war orphan.

All around me, the dry grass whines with heat. Above, a hawk glides in the sky, and on a rock nearby, a lizard basks in the hot sun. Ellie's no war orphan, but her bad moods can put her on the warpath, as the phone call showed. What's she so sour about? I get the feeling she's coming out here this weekend with an agenda: maybe to settle a score, maybe to steal the show. Who knows.

I hear the crunch of gravel, and turn to see Gabe huffing toward me on his bike. Actually I shouldn't say huffing. Gabe's resting heart rate is fifty-five, which is good, and during a workout it'll get up to maybe one-fifty-five, which is great, and within five minutes after stopping it's right back down to where it started, which is disgusting. Gabe doesn't believe in bicycle helmets and instead wears a red bandanna around his forehead to catch the sweat.

Straddling his bike, he wipes his forehead and hocks something jelly-like into the trees. The lizard skitters off. 'Your dad called,' he tells me. 'His plane just left, so we've got until two at least. Come on, we'll take the bikes down to Eldorado.'

It occurs to me that perhaps Ellie is still miffed that I never told Gabe about the money she lent me. Maybe as part of her agenda, she plans to let it drop this weekend. Well, fine. I've been meaning to tell him for a long time anyway.

'Hey Gabe,' I say, 'you know when I paid off some of our medical bills last year?'

'What medical bills?'

Man oh man, this guy knows nothing. 'The Clomid injections?'

'Oh,' he says. 'Right. So?'

'Didn't you ever wonder like where I got the money?'

'No,' he said. 'What'd you do, rob a bank?'

'Well, no,' and I tell him about Ellie's loan. There. Said and done.

Gabe says, 'You paid her back, right?'

'No.'

'Nothing at all?'

I glance away. Why was it suddenly so important to tell him, now of all times?

'How much are we talking about here?' he asks.

'Not that much. Hey, let's go. Were you thinking of doing the whole canyon?'

'How much, Isabel?'

'Well,' I say, 'around ten thousand.'

With thumb and middle finger, Gabe wipes the corners of his mouth. 'That's kind of dishonest, isn't it?'

'Well, it wasn't really a lie,' I begin.

'Sorry?'

'Okay, okay,' I say quickly. 'It was a kind of lie. But I'm telling you now, so that's telling the truth.'

Gabe squats down on a rock, pulls up a stalk of grass, and bites the end. 'I like this.'

'What?'

'Having you on the spot like this.'

'Are you mad?'

'Yes I'm mad.'

'How mad?'

'Pretty mad,' he says. 'Is there anything else I should know before Ellie gets here?'

'No.'

'You're sure? No other checks?'

'No.'

'Good.'

I look deep into his eyes, searching for the golden fleck, hoping for some marital welfare here. He gazes back. 'You're pretty nervous about this, aren't you?'

'I wasn't five minutes ago, but I am now,' I say. 'You're right, it was a lie. It was stupid.'

'Remember how you were afraid to tell me the truth about your mother?'

'Yes.'

'That really pissed me off.'

'I know. So if you wanted to make a big deal over this, no one would blame you.'

Gabe picks up a rock and sends it sailing out over the hillside. 'But you're wrong, Isabel. I'd blame myself. Do you think I want to rev things up again over something like this? I had a shitty summer, Isabel. I felt lost. I felt empty. I felt like there was no point to anything, without you. I don't want to go back to that. I could make a big deal out of this, sure. I could say you deceived me. I could say I couldn't trust you again, ever. But you know what? I don't believe any of that. I think this is just one of those things. You fuck up. You fix things. You go on. Am I right?'

I clear my throat.

'Tell me this,' he says. 'Have we got the money to pay her back now?'

'We'll find it,' I tell him. 'We'll pay her a little each month.'

'How much did all those injections cost, anyway?'

'Around thirty thousand.'

'We were pretty out of control, weren't we?'

It angers me to hear him adopt such a judgmental tone. Maybe he feels more rational now, but if I had to do it all over again, I'd still jump through all those hoops.

'We've never even called an adoption agency,' he says. 'Shouldn't we get on it? Doesn't it take a couple of years?'

He's right. All this time I've studiously avoided even opening the phone book. 'Monday,' I say. 'But you have to call, too. I'm not doing all the work.'

'I put up with so much,' he complains.

★ ★ ★

The first time my mother tried to kill herself she was thirty-six. It was a Saturday, and it was late winter. There was a gray misty drizzle outside, and my father was going to take me and Ellie to the zoo.

He took us to the zoo on Saturdays because it got us all out of the house, and an empty house was something my mother needed like some people need phone lines, or television sets, or sunshine. A dose of solitude. My father would pack a lunch and we'd pile into the Plymouth and drive along Lake Washington, up over the ship canal, past the university and on to the zoo.

71

Usually we spent most of our time in the monkey house, fascinated and horrified by the occasional red erection that poked out like a tongue. After lunch we would go downtown to my father's office, located high up in the Smith Tower, where we would watch the wide-waked ferries toiling across the bay.

Then we would head on home. This was the hard part of the day, because it was my dream that my mother would be in the kitchen with an apron around her waist, humming as she peeled potatoes, fried hamburgers, and tore lettuce leaves into a wooden bowl. Yet I knew that in reality we would return to a dark, silent house that smelled of cigarettes. More often than not my mother would be upstairs in her bedroom, smoking and playing solitaire. Sometimes she had a drink going. Sometimes she was already asleep. My father would settle Ellie and me before the television and heat up a can of ravioli, and we'd eat, without my mother, in front of the TV.

'How was your day with Daddy?' she would say, when we tiptoed in to kiss her good night. 'Did you have fun at the zoo? Did you get some cotton candy? I love the zoo. But go to sleep now. We've got a busy day tomorrow.'

She made it sound like we had family plans. We never had family plans, not to speak of, anyway.

That awful drizzly day was just like the other zoo days, only after the zoo we went to the movies instead of my father's office. When we got out of the theater it was already dark, and the city streets glistened black and slick. Driving up the back alley, my father said he was ready for a good fire and a glass of Scotch, and we could all watch Lawrence Welk. I just wanted a bath — preferably with bubbles, and preferably with my mother kneeling beside the tub, squeezing hot water on my back.

My father parked the car in front of the garage. We never parked either of our cars inside the garage, because it was too small — maybe wide enough to get the car in, but you'd never be able to open the doors. Mostly we used the garage for storage — garden tools and suitcases, a stack of boxes from my mother's college days, an old refrigerator that froze everything solid.

We all got out of the car and Ellie and I elbowed each other to get to the kitchen door first. The house was dark. Our father nudged us aside, inserted his key, turned and pushed. The door would not open.

'Hurry, I'm freezing,' Ellie said.

'I call the first bath.'

'I called it this morning.'

'Oh, you are such a liar!'

'Girls.' My father held up his keys to the light, then tried unlocking the door again. Still the key turned, but the door seemed stuck. He squeezed his way behind the camellia bush over to the kitchen window and cupped his hands against the glass to peer inside.

There are some sounds, like a music box, or your mother's low laughter in the middle of the night, that you will never forget. For me it is the sound of breaking glass. My father made a choking sound. He tried to open the window but it wouldn't budge, and he shouted, 'Get back, get back!' as he threw his shoulder against the window. I can still hear the sound of glass shards raining on the tile floor inside — it seemed to go on forever, that liquid tinkling sound, and then my father hoisted himself up and climbed in through the window frame, groaning like a beast. He landed with a thud and we could hear glass crunching underfoot, furniture being shoved about, and then the door flew open and my father came wobbling backwards, dragging my mother by the armpits.

When I opened my eyes, my father was crouched on the ground, cradling my mother's head against his chest. She was mumbling, and when she opened her eyes and saw me and Ellie, she put her hands over her face. My father told us to go inside. Ellie took my hand and we went into the house. There was glass all over the kitchen floor, and dirty dishes everywhere, but apart from that I couldn't tell what exactly had happened to my mother. Ellie led me into the living room and turned on Lawrence Welk and we sat side by side on the sofa, waiting.

I came up with some pretty creative theories while watching the Lennon Sisters that night. My mother had smoked too many cigarettes and they put her to sleep. She'd eaten too much. Drank too much. Was simply exhausted.

In the end, nobody had to explain anything to me. I didn't have any hard facts, and didn't learn about the pills until later, but I knew that what had happened hadn't been any accident. My father wouldn't say anything about it except that my mother was lucky we came home when we did. I didn't see her as lucky. I saw her go off in the ambulance with a mask over her face and a needle in her arm, and nothing about her situation seemed very lucky to me.

For the first time in our lives, our father left us alone that night, so he could go with our mother to the hospital. Ellie and I took a bath together, turning the heater on full blast and filling the tub to our chests. We washed our hair, and we washed each other's backs, and finally, when our fingers were all wrinkled and the water was cloudy with soap, we climbed out and toweled each other off. We put on Nana's flannel nighties and combed each other's hair out, and climbed into Ellie's bed, where she started reading a Nancy Drew mystery to me. She read chapter after chapter until she finished the book, and then she started another one, because we just couldn't sleep.

★ ★ ★

The next day my mother came home with a carton of donuts from the grocery store. She wore a clean gray skirt and a red cardigan, and if you ignored the blue kerchief she looked like any mother out to bring home a Sunday treat for her family before church. She sat down at the kitchen table, opened the box of donuts, and greedily wolfed down three in a row, licking powdered sugar off her fingers. She told us the food in the hospital was terrible, and she hadn't eaten anything since breakfast the day before. After she ate her donuts, she said she was tired, and went upstairs and lay down, and ended up sleeping the rest of the day. My father said it was her medicine, which he now kept in his pocket, as closely guarded as a vial of gold.

8

Back at the house, Gabe loads the bikes onto the car and I fill the water bottles. We drive down the mountain and into town along the main artery. There is a carnival going on in our city park today, with white tents and craft booths and kiddie rides. We continue up past the university, past more tree-lined subdivisions, and head out of town through sloping, tawny meadows, where cows graze and pockets of yellow cottonwoods shimmer in the late summer light. Off to the west, the rocky Flatirons and the cliffs of Eldorado Canyon rise high in the china-blue sky.

We park at the base of the canyon. High above, on steep, glistening walls, climbers inch their way upward. We get on our bikes and pedal nonstop to the top of the canyon, then zoom down again, and end up at the old pool, where we dive into icy waters that just this morning spilled down from the Continental Divide.

Drying off in the sun, I manage to empty my mind of dark thoughts concerning the visit. But when during the drive home Gabe asks what I want to do for dinner tonight, it all comes back. I am mildly annoyed he hasn't figured out the dinner arrangements yet, and say as much, this being my birthday after all. He reminds me there wasn't a lot of notice and besides, who can cook for my sister with all her dietary restrictions? He's right. Ellie doesn't eat any meat, dairy, shellfish, refined sugar, or peanuts. Gabe wishes out loud that Wilson were coming, since Wilson eats anything. 'If Wilson were coming, there'd be no place for Rachel to sleep,' I remind him. He shrugs. Easy menus have priority for Gabe.

It shouldn't be any surprise that Wilson is not coming. In the nine years he's been married to Ellie, I've seen him face to face five times, I believe. Usually he's too busy with his business — whatever business it is that allows him six months in the south of France every year. Just exactly what he does, nobody knows, and Ellie doesn't help when she refers to the third tax audit in as many years, or the fact that he was in Jakarta, Miami, and Geneva in one week alone. On the other hand, he's not a bad husband, or a bad father. He pays twenty thousand dollars a year for Ellie's therapy without batting an eye. He gave her the best room in the apartment to use as a studio. He sends her off to Paris for a month of art lessons while he takes Rachel camel-riding in Morocco. He coaches Rachel's soccer team and volunteers in her classroom and organizes field trips. All things considered, he's a decent guy.

Even if he isn't up front about everything.

★ ★ ★

It's two o'clock when we pull into our driveway. I'd figured on at least half an hour before anyone arrived, but there in our driveway sits a white Land Cruiser, and from the open windows of our living room comes the sound of piano music.

My father plays only by ear. This means if you give him a sheet of music, he'll struggle clumsily through a few bars, squinting and frowning; but soon he'll give up, close his eyes, and play the songs he hears in his head, sultry riffs in a minor key which float away like dandelion fluff. Back in Seattle we had an old upright, and he would play late at night, when everyone was in bed. As my mother got closer to the end, he played even more, and I would go to bed on those nights with his music wrapped around my heart. It was something to grab onto, something that made me feel safe, even if my mother did happen to be locked in the bathroom burning her wrists with cigarettes.

But after her death he stopped, and those hours before falling asleep were some of the quietest and most anguished hours of my life. Images of a happy young woman hovered above me as I tried to fall asleep. My mother in her pedal pushers planting daffodils, tying her red scarf on a cool summer morning, driving through wheat fields, dancing in the rain late at night. Some nights it was so bad I put my pillow over my head and hummed one note, just for the noise.

Anyway, hearing his music makes me feel stitched up right now, and I could sit here forever, just listening. But as soon as Gabe slams the car door, the music stops. In a moment my father appears on the deck.

'Howdy do,' he says.

Even though it's close to ninety-five degrees, he's wearing pressed khakis and a white button-down shirt. 'There's my birthday girl,' he says, coming to meet me on the steps. 'Happy birthday, sweetheart.'

He is warm and smells of chocolate and wool. His neck is damp, his shoulders wide and solid beneath my hands. We hold onto each other for that extra second, that extra pulse. Then he clears his throat and pulls back.

'Gabriel,' he says, reaching out to grasp Gabe's hand.

'Hugh,' says Gabe. 'Good to have you here.'

'Good to finally be here!' my father exclaims. 'Had the toughest time with the rental place because they lost my darn reservation! Where've you been?'

'Swimming,' I say. 'Have you been here long?'

'Twenty minutes. Your refrigerator isn't very cold,' he tells me. 'When's the last time you vacuumed out the coils? You wouldn't believe what I found. You really want to pay a service guy sixty bucks to come and suck up a little dust?'

'No, Dad.'

'Keep up your house,' my father scolds. 'Where's Ellie?'

'Not here yet. Why?'

'Because she should be here! Her plane was supposed to get in before mine! Darn that girl,' and he frowns at the ground.

'Maybe she's having trouble with the rental agency, too,' Gabe offers.

My father asks, 'Have you heard anything at all from her?'

I look at Gabe. 'What was it, ten o'clock? She

80

called from the plane. We didn't talk too long because Rachel was upset over something.'

'Rachel!' my father exclaims. 'Rachel wasn't supposed to come! Rachel's coming?'

'What did you expect?'

'Why, just the three of us. Four, I mean — sorry, Gabe. Shoot, I love my granddaughter as much as anyone but I thought this would be an adult weekend. Gosh, that kid has a lot of energy!'

My father is a widower twice over now, and he likes his peace and quiet. Which he has a lot of these days. Twenty years after my mother died, he married a woman named Suzanne, a woman who was calm, who called my father 'Hugh dear,' who ate well-balanced meals and wrote thankyou notes on monogrammed stationery — in short, the opposite of my mother. Everything was swell for a while. Then she got cancer.

'Gabe'll baby-sit,' I say. 'We'll have plenty of time for just the three of us. You'll take care of Rachel, won't you, Gabe?'

'Me?' says Gabe, stricken.

My father looks at his watch. 'Gosh darn her.'

'Come on inside,' I tell him. 'Get out of those hot clothes. You want a beer or something? Glass of wine?'

'Just water,' he says. 'Darn that girl.'

Again I tell my father not to worry, but five minutes later, standing under the cool spray in the shower, I find myself equally fretful, though for different reasons. Maybe my sister wasn't on a plane to Denver. All the old images come back. I see her getting off another plane in some

81

equatorial country with a wide-brimmed hat, large round sunglasses, a fake passport and a purse full of pills. I see her bicycling across the Golden Gate Bridge and stopping midway and then, when nobody is looking, nimbly hopping the rail and free-falling into the choppy waters below. I see her stepping off the edge of a subway platform, or checking into a hotel with a pack of safety razors.

By the time I turn off the water, a prickly rash has spread across my stomach.

9

The reason my father and I get so worried whenever Ellie doesn't show is because she's been known to run away more than once. Like that time in college, when she called up threatening to drive her car into a lake. When your sister calls and says she's going to drive her car into the lake, you think of your mother in her Dodge Dart and tell yourself you're not going to take any chances. Which is why I called the police — I was three thousand miles away and my sister had just hung up on me from a pay phone in a donut shop with her car engine idling outside. I saw the road, I saw the lake. I saw the whole night unfold, and I called the police. Big mistake, but only in hindsight. How was I supposed to know she didn't mean it at the time? Or that the arrival of the police would send her off into hiding?

For a month Ellie refused to talk to us or let us come visit her at the retreat. It was winter, and I was a sophomore at the University of Washington at the time, living at home with my father. We spent mornings talking with the doctors back in New Hampshire, and they told us Ellie was making progress but we shouldn't try and push things. Instead, we should just be supportive. That always bugged me. How can you be supportive when nobody will clue you in on what's wrong?

One day I came home and found a letter addressed to me, in Ellie's handwriting. Expecting a long, contemplative explanation, I found instead one of those tall narrow humor cards, with a frazzled woman on the cover and a weak pun inside about running out of thyme.

Dear Izzy,
This card made me think of you, don't ask why, Ha! Ha! Long time no see. I am the basket queen of the White Mountains. Elavil makes you sleepy. But I am doing fine. Trust you are too. Say hi to Pop. Don't worry, no lakes nearby. Just a joke!
— Ellie

That night my father and I quarreled, with me insisting that the letter was an implicit invitation and him convinced that we should wait for something more direct. I finally persuaded him by pointing out that sisters know sisters better than fathers know daughters, and the next day I flew to Boston, rented a car, and drove north for three hours.

It was dusk when I pulled into the parking lot of the retreat. Built of white clapboards, it looked like a rambling one-story house, with add-on wings reaching out into the surrounding woodland. ('Units,' Ellie would later correct me. 'I'm in Unit D. D for Depressed.') Crusty snow mottled the grounds, which had been landscaped with clusters of birch trees and granite boulders and pebble paths looping to nowhere.

Inside the main entrance, my sister awaited my arrival. She was wearing a black leotard and a long, droopy black skirt, with black socks and no shoes. Her long hair seemed oily and unwashed; she'd twisted it into a barrette against the back of her head, and she had lost so much weight that her cheekbones stuck out and her eyes had a sunken, hollow look to them, as though haunted by some malignant spirit.

She smiled and held open her arms. As I hugged her fragile frame, I thought that if I hugged too hard, she would break in half.

'Bellissima,' she said. 'What a good little sister you are, to come and visit me like this.' She took my arm and led me down the hall, showed me her room with its unmade bed pushed flat against the wall, the gleaming bathrooms, the arts and crafts center that smelled of glue. She pointed out the wing where the doctors' offices were, but told me we couldn't go down there.

'If you stay a few days, you can probably meet my doctor. He's very cool except I think he's attracted to me,' Ellie said. 'And since he's married, I don't think I should sleep with him. Do you have any Chap Stick?'

I rummaged through my purse.

'I've slept with five married men,' Ellie went on, reaching up to reclasp her barrette. 'They all said their wives wouldn't give them blow jobs. When I get married,' she declared, 'I'm going to give great head. You're not a virgin, are you?'

I was a sophomore in college, I'd never had a boyfriend, and I lived at home with my father. So yes, I was a virgin.

'God, no,' I laughed.

'Good,' Ellie said, 'because if you were, you'd never understand anything I'm going through. Here,' she said, opening a set of French doors to the dining room, 'we can sit down.' There were round polished tables and captain's chairs, with white cafe curtains in the window. It reminded me of the restaurant near Mount Rainier; all it lacked was an orangeade cooler and a waitress named Joyce.

'Does the reason you're here have anything to do with the married men?' I asked, thinking that romantic pain could lead any fragile twenty-one-year-old to drive her car into a lake.

'Oh Lord no,' she said, pulling out a chair for herself. 'They were all just for fun. See, the doctors think something horrendous happened to me that I can't remember — and it's not Mother, because I can remember Mother — isn't that funny? You'd sure think it'd be about Mother, wouldn't you? — but they say Mother's not it and if I talk about things enough, then I'll remember. A plus B will equal C.'

'So once you remember, you won't want to kill yourself anymore?'

Ellie lit a cigarette. 'Blunt blunt blunt, aren't we?'

I couldn't hide my fury. 'What do you think we've been going through? You think it's easy getting that kind of a phone call? You think it's easy waiting around for the repeat performance?'

'I was never really going to do it,' she said cheerfully. 'I'm too much of a wimp. I mean, just look at me!' She straightened up, as if on display.

86

'I can't stand blood so I can't slit my wrists. I'm afraid of a coma so I won't swallow pills. Guns are too messy, and they confiscated my car. So for heaven's sake don't worry.'

I didn't say that from the way she was talking, I was going to worry for the rest of my life.

'What do you talk about with your doctor?' I asked.

'Off limits,' she said sharply.

'Even to your sister?'

'It's still off limits,' she said, and there was a prim note in her voice that suggested a duty to keep secrets, even her own. 'Don't be nosy. What you don't know won't hurt you. Want some M&Ms?'

I left my sister that night with a promise to bring cherry-flavored Chap Stick the next morning. A few miles down the road I found a motel. I checked in, took a shower, climbed into bed, and debated what to tell my father. When I finally made the call, I felt too protective to tell him the truth. She's doing fine, I told him. Good. Great, in fact.

'She could be conning you,' he warned. 'Your mother was a great con artist.'

'Not always so great,' I pointed out. 'We all knew.'

'Not all the time,' he sighed.

The next day I met several doctors, including Ellie's, and while they all struck me as sympathetic and wise, I found it difficult to hold their gaze for very long. I had the feeling they were judging me, and using me to judge Ellie, even as we talked about such banalities as the rain in Seattle. Ellie's doctor was a short, stubby man with thinning gray hair, and I detected nothing in his manner that suggested he might be attracted to Ellie in any inappropriate way. I wondered, as I so often did, how much of anything I could believe.

We ate lunch in the dining room, where I met some of her friends. There was a woman from Maine with scars on her wrists. An older woman who kept checking her watch against the clock above the doorway. A young man, maybe Ellie's age, with lonely deep-set eyes and large ears and long fingers. Ellie told me he was a music major at Boston University. 'Acid laced with strychnine,' she whispered, when he went back to the milk machine for a refill. 'A very bad trip. Hey, Ron,' she said gently as he sat back down. 'Did you see the desserts?'

Ron smiled faintly. 'There's dessert?'

'Chocolate cake,' Ellie said.

'Yum,' he said.

Ellie barely touched her soup, but she had two pieces of cake. When everyone else had left, she was still pressing crumbs with her index finger and licking them off greedily. 'These people are so sweet,' she said. 'Don't you think?'

No, I didn't. I didn't think they were sweet at all, I thought they were all very, very disturbed, and I hated to see my sister among them.

'How long are you going to be here?' I asked.

'Oh, I don't know,' Ellie said. 'They don't say. Maybe a few months.'

'Ellie,' I said, 'do you know why these other people are here?'

88

'Same reason I am,' Ellie said, applying Chap Stick. 'We're loony.'

'You're not loony.'

'Well, what can I say. I guess I'm just here because my life is a piece of shit.'

'Why?' I demanded.

Ellie glanced over her shoulder, then took a half-crushed cigarette from her hip pocket, slipped it between her lips, and cupped a match to it. 'The sixty-four-thousand-dollar question,' she said, blowing smoke rings. 'Answer it and we're set for life, aren't we?'

Older sisters always get the last word. I didn't have anything to say to that. My sister's life wasn't a piece of shit at all, as far as I could see. Then again, neither was my mother's, on the surface, so maybe I was born missing the obvious.

I left early the next day. I told myself it was good that I came, that Ellie appreciated the visit. But I was glad to go. I was glad to leave her in the care of doctors who would see through her lies, glad that there were no razors in the building, that the pharmaceuticals were all locked up, that nobody had a car or access to the roof. Glad, too, that if my sister's creative mind were to come up with some heretofore unknown manner by which to try and kill herself again, there were buckles and belts and pills and round-the-clock doctors, round-the-clock aides, to pick up the pieces and put them back together again. It didn't have to be me.

★   ★   ★

Yet it's not always Ellie with the problem and me with my act together. During the months after our mother's death, it was me who woke up crying in the night, and Ellie who took me into her bed and lulled me to sleep. It was Ellie who boxed up my mother's clothes and took them to the thrift shop, Ellie who took on the grocery shopping, Ellie who dug out the Christmas decorations and strung the house with lights that first year so that we could pretend to be festive. If I got sick, Ellie stayed home from school and made me tea and cinnamon toast. She knew instinctively what to do, when I needed it.

Even later she was there for me: when I fell apart over a bad love affair, for instance, or when I kept getting my period after the Clomid injections. Clearly I've had my moments. The difference between us is that I only cry when there is something to cry about. I have never seen a shrink and never had insomnia. I have never needed medication. I have never thought of driving my car into a lake.

Sometimes I'm so sane it makes me sick.

10

The crunch of tires, two quick honks, and a car door slamming shut — it's three-thirty and finally, surprise, there is my sister slinging a black duffel over her shoulder as she unfolds from the car. She is wearing cut-offs and a loose black tank that reveals an utter lack of any bosom whatsoever. And there, too, is my niece Rachel, although I can only see her through the window, where she remains scrunched down in the front seat.

Ellie squints as she toils up the steps to the deck. A golden stud gleams on her left nostril, and when she shades her brow I can make out bruised moons of loose skin beneath her eyes.

'I swear I always forget about the goddamn altitude,' she says, dropping her duffel at my feet. 'Isn't it a little on the hot side for a mile above sea level? Hug,' she demands, holding her arms out to me. 'Mmmm, you smell like Nana, like oldish. Just kidding, dear.' She breaks away and surveys the stumps and rocks and tufts of cheatgrass that constitute our yard. 'Are you ever going to put some plants in around here or do you like living in a dog pen?'

'One of these days,' I say.

'Is Dad here yet?'

'Dad!' I shout. 'Hey Dad! Of course he's here,' I say. 'Why are you late?'

My sister holds the bridge of her nose and lets

a spasm pass through. 'Long story,' she says. 'I'll go into it later. Rachel!' she shouts at the car. 'Rachel, stop pouting! And carry the cake up when you come, all right? Rachel is mad,' Ellie tells me, 'because I won't let her put green mascara in her hair.'

This from the woman who has done everything possible to her own head of hair? I'll keep my mouth shut on this one. In a minute the passenger door opens, and a reluctant Rachel climbs out in an oversized pink T-shirt. She wears glasses now, and they make her look chubby, especially with that bubble of orange ringlets. She slams the front door, opens the back door, and lifts out a large white bakery box.

'Careful,' Ellie calls down, and then aside to me, 'Something happened in the last year — physical grace, forget it. Sometimes I just have to wonder if they got Wilson's sperm mixed up with Chevy Chase's. Watch the steps, hon,' she warns as Rachel starts up the stairs to the deck. She rests her chin on the top of the box and feels with her feet for each step and finally makes it to the top, where Ellie takes the box and sets it on the table.

'Say hello,' she prods. 'Remember your manners.'

'Hello, Aunt Izzy,' Rachel says, then immediately tugs at Ellie's shorts.

'What?'

Rachel whispers into Ellie's ear. Ellie sighs. 'So go find the bathroom,' she says.

Rachel whispers again. Ellie looks at her

sternly. Rachel turns and walks stiffly into the house.

'It's right by the kitchen,' I call after her.

Ellie watches her daughter reprovingly. 'She's gotten so shy,' she complains. 'We're really working on this right now. Where's Dad, anyway? Yo Hugh! Hugh my man, I'm here! Where is he, anyway?'

'Gabe's showing him his new computer. They're online.'

'I like the sex and violence sites myself,' Ellie says. 'How hot is it, anyway? It feels like the fucking Sahara desert. I can't take heat these days, you know? I'm perimenopausal. Can't you do something about this?'

I am happy to see my sister. Happy as the dickens, in fact, to look into her speckled green eyes and smell her smells, buttery and limy and slightly unwashed. She holds onto my shoulder and kicks off her sandals, glancing up as Gabe steps out onto the deck.

'Hey,' he says. 'When'd you get in?'

'Just now,' says Ellie, 'and it's been a very long trip. I like the earring,' she tells him.

Gabe fingers his ear lobe.

'Now this thing hurt way more than I expected,' she tells us, touching the gold stud. 'And then, even though I swabbed my nose with so much alcohol it felt like a chemical peel, I get the worst sinus infection you can imagine. And on top of it, now Rachel wants one too. So much for being impulsive, huh?'

'We're on fire alert, by the way,' Gabe tells her.

'Groovy groovy,' Ellie says. 'So what?'

'In case you need to smoke,' he explains.

'I quit,' Ellie says, 'but thanks for the reminder. Oh, don't get excited, Isabel, I quit all the time. Should I have sunscreen on right now do you think? Doesn't the sun out here give you cancer like in two minutes?'

Gabe murmurs something about smoking.

'What's that, Gabe?'

'Nothing,' Gabe says.

'Shouldn't I worry about lung cancer, is that what you said? Of course I should. And I do, believe me. I worry about every kind of cancer there is,' Ellie says. 'I don't need reminding.'

'It was a joke,' Gabe says.

'Bad joke,' Ellie says. 'For a hypochondriac.'

There's an awkward silence. Gabe clears his throat. 'By the way, at some point this weekend we should talk about the money we owe you.'

Ellie turns, and allows me a dignified nod of approval. 'No shit, Isabel, sometimes you impress the hell out of me. When did you break it to him?'

'Actually, I've known for some time,' Gabe tells her.

'Yeah, like a couple of hours, I bet. What, Izzy — you thought I might blab?' She gives me a gentle punch on the arm. 'Probably a good move on your part, since discretion is not one of my better qualities.'

'To return to the issue,' Gabe says, 'I just want you to know that we'll pay you back, over time.'

'It was a gift, Gabe darling.'

'Even so.'

Ellie shrugs. 'Sounds like a guy thing to me.

94

God, I hate quitting smoking. Why did I choose this month?'

At that point my father steps out onto the deck, closing the sliding door behind him so as not to waste cool air. 'What's this about smoking?'

'Hi Daddy,' Ellie says, sliding her arm around his waist. He squeezes her shoulder.

'You put on any weight since our last visit?' he asks gruffly.

'Five pounds,' Ellie says.

'It doesn't look like five pounds. What took you so long, anyway? Plane late?'

'Long story,' she says with a gingery sigh. 'Just be glad I'm here.'

'I am,' he says, squeezing her shoulder again. 'Although I wish you'd told me beforehand about bringing Rachel.'

'Like she's a problem?'

'I just like to know the game plan ahead of time, honey,' my father says. 'You know me. Back to my question, though — I thought you quit smoking a long time ago.'

'I did, Dad,' Ellie says. 'Relax. Jeez. This is supposed to be a party weekend. Rachel!' she calls. 'Come out here and say hello to your grandfather! I'll have to warn you,' she tells our father, 'Rachel is in a very bratty stage right now and she'll spend most of the weekend monopolizing the conversation. If you get tired of listening to her, just tell her to shut up. Not those words, of course, but tell her it's time to be quiet, because if you don't, she'll give you the complete history of every single Pokémon that ever lived.'

'Pokémon?'

'You don't want to know,' Ellie sighs. 'Which also reminds me. Whatever you do, don't let her talk you into taking her to a toy store. Whenever Wilson's parents come into the city, it's FAO this, FAO that. They don't know how to say no. Not like me, anyway. I'm very very good at saying no — right, honey?' She is looking over my shoulder, and we follow her gaze. Rachel has cracked open the sliding door and is gesturing wildly for Ellie to come inside — although as soon as she sees us looking at her, she halts and forces a smile.

'Out,' Ellie commands. Rachel steps out onto the deck.

'Say hello to Grampa,' Ellie tells Rachel.

'Hi, Grampa,' Rachel says.

Ellie cocks her head. 'Hello, not hi.'

'Hello, Grampa.'

'Hello, Rachel my dear,' my father says, giving a slight bow, and he sneaks in a little wink, too, that only Rachel and I see, signaling that he couldn't care less whether his granddaughter says hi, or hey, or whatever.

'You should see what Uncle Gabe has,' Rachel tells her mother. 'Parachutes in his ceiling! And a whole wall full of dolls!'

'Rachel,' Ellie says, catching my eye, 'I'm not sure a parachute can be *in* a ceiling. Do you mean the parachutes are hanging *from* the ceiling?'

'Parachutes and hang gliders,' Rachel says. 'It is so cool. Come and see!'

I tell Rachel that if she asks nicely, Gabe might show her how a hang glider works tomorrow morning. Then I ask if she's hungry. She is, and my father declares that now he could use a beer, and Ellie says if she doesn't get into the shower she is going to wear the smell of buffalo balls in her hair for the entire weekend since the guy sitting next to her on the plane from Dallas was a buffalo farmer and smelled like he'd slept curled up in the groin of a dead bull for the last month.

'Good choice of words, Ellie hon,' my father remarks.

'I liked him,' Rachel says. 'He gave me his dessert.'

'Ever had a Fat Tire, Dad?' I ask.

'What the heck is that?'

'It's a kind of beer, Dad. You'll like it.'

Ellie says, 'I'll take a Fat Tire, but if I don't wash I'm not kidding I am going to puke. Come sit with me, Izzie, I need some adult company.'

My sister and I collect her bags and head down to the lower level, where she and Rachel will be sleeping. It's cooler here. Our guest room is furnished with pieces from Seattle — the four-poster beds that Nana eventually bought for Ellie and me, the white wicker chair from our living room, and our mother's glossy mahogany bureau. On it sits a photograph of her, taken a year or so before she died. She is sitting at the top of the forty-nine steps with a bottle of Coke in one hand, a cigarette in the other, smiling broadly.

I watch my sister as she throws her duffel on one of the beds, unzips it and digs through her

97

clothes for a bottle of shampoo. She chatters about the traffic on the way to LaGuardia and how muggy it was in New York, still, and how good it is for Rachel to see how I live (read: Aunt Izzy is not rich), and I feel hopeful for the weekend, hopeful that as a family we will come together and toast my forty-one years and look back upon all that happened so long ago with the wisdom of gods.

'Thanks for coming. I'm glad you're here,' I tell her. 'Be nice to Gabe, though. Don't pick on him. Let him pay you back. And if you don't mind let's stay away from the baby issues, all right? No I'm not pregnant. No we're not going to do in vitro. Yes we might adopt. Enough said?'

Ellie stands before the mirror over the bureau and examines a freckle on her temple. 'Well, I'm glad I'm here too, and not just because New York is a sauna.'

'Why were you late?'

Ellie does not answer. She pads down the hall to the bathroom, where she strips off her clothes and drops them in a meager pile on the tile floor and turns on the shower. At forty-three she still has the body of a boy, with pelvic bones that poke out like extra ears under her skin. They are so prominent you could grab hold of them and lift her up over your head, easy.

'I'm waiting,' I say.

Ellie sticks her hand into the spray, then steps behind the shower curtain. 'Wilson's gone to France,' she calls out.

'So what? You have a house in France.'

'Yes, we do at that. But usually we don't buy one-way tickets.'

I wait for her to clarify, but all I hear is the spray of water.

'As in what, divorce?' I mean it as a joke, but Ellie does not answer. 'Please tell me you're kidding,' I say.

'Wish I were,' Ellie calls out. 'Don't use the D-word in front of Miss Rachel, though. Miss Rachel's flipped out. Miss Rachel had a tantrum this morning in her bedroom, which is why we were late getting to the airport, which is why we missed our direct flight and had to stop in Dallas, where Rachel got sick and threw up all over me. Then!' she exclaims, 'after throwing up she had an asthma attack, so I gave her a squirt from the inhaler, but that didn't touch it and did I pack the Epi-pen? No I did not, given the rush this morning, so we now have to get her off the airplane and find First Aid, where they give her a shot of epinephrine and insist on observing her for an hour. The plane leaves, we have to find a new connection. That's why we're a little late,' she finishes.

It's a good story, although I sense it's incomplete. 'Whose idea was this?'

'You mean who's dumping whom? Me him. Do you ever get these things?'

'What things?'

'Come here,' she says, and naturally I obey: parting the shower curtain, I see her feeling her groin. 'These things,' she says, and she takes my fingers and places them against the hollow at the top of her thigh and moves them in a little circle.

99

'They're your lymph nodes,' I tell her. 'They're BB's. They're fine.'

'They feel kind of big to me,' she says doubtfully.

'That's because you're too skinny. Are you throwing up again?'

'They're not peas?'

'They're not peas, they're BB's,' I say. 'How come you didn't tell me this was happening?'

'What, about the divorce? Well Christ, I didn't think he'd actually go.'

'I thought you said it was your decision.'

Ellie shuts off the water, steps out and wraps herself in a towel. 'It was, and don't tell Dad. Don't tell Gabe, either.'

My sister has always done this, told me things on condition of secrecy, conditions I honored all through our childhood and indeed into college — until the night she said she was driving her car into the lake. Don't tell Dad, she said, and I promised, then hung up and told my father the entire story.

'Because I'm just fine with this,' Ellie continues. 'I am not going to go jumping out of any windows, I am not going to go driving into any lakes. I don't even need to up my dosage. I'll get the apartment, and I'll get the house in Vermont, and I'll get Rachel. Wilson can have everything else.'

How long has she been here, all of twenty minutes? What other bombs does she have? And she is fine with this the way I was fine every time I got my period when we were trying to get pregnant. I see Wilson's departure releasing a swarm of bees in her head.

'Don't be so judgmental, Izzy,' Ellie says. 'Just because you have the perfect marriage.'

'I didn't say that.'

'You're thinking it, though.'

No I'm not. What I'm thinking is, who's going to take care of you now, with Wilson out of the picture? Wilson was a goddamn saint, when it came to taking care of you.

'And I can take care of myself just fine,' Ellie says. 'I'm not who I used to be. Besides, things will actually be easier now, with Wilson gone. Living with Wilson was no picnic, you know.'

'No, I didn't know that,' I say, 'since you never tell me very much about Wilson.'

Ellie leans toward the mirror and stretches down the purplish circles underneath her eyes. 'Well, he's quite volatile, and I'll just leave it at that. I'm glad to move on, actually,' she says breezily. 'Maybe without Wilson, my life can finally get back to normal.'

I don't think Ellie's life has ever been normal, but maybe that's not what we should be worrying about, just now.

'Look at this stomach,' Ellie says. 'I'm so fat.'

I stare at her.

She stands back and catches my eye in the mirror. 'It was just a joke,' she says. 'God, Izzy, you're so serious.'

11

A normal life. To me as a girl, it was a concept like heaven — a nice idea, but a fairy tale at its core. Not that we didn't strive for one. We decorated a Christmas tree in December and hunted for eggs in April and lit off sparklers on the Fourth of July; once in a while we took a family hike, or rode our bikes together.

In one of our grander efforts, we got a dog. I was eight and Ellie was ten — a good age, my mother said, not so young that she herself would have to do all the work, but not so old that we would be more interested in boys. My father suggested that we get a cat, but my mother looked at him as though he had just revealed a major character flaw. A cat? God, Hugh.

As usual, my parents bickered over what kind of dog to get, with my father wanting a golden retriever and my mother insisting on a mutt. Anything pedigreed would be too rambunctious, she maintained. For weeks the issue remained unresolved, until one day, when my father was at work, Ellie and I came home from school to find our mother waiting with her coat buttoned, her scarf tied. 'I'm going down to the pound to see what they have,' she said brightly. 'Want to come?'

I had heard about the pound, how they took in strays and gassed them in a little white room. I thought it would be heroic of us to save a dog from such a fate.

We went to the pound, and they took us back into the kennels to show us the litter they'd just received. There in the far corner of a concrete pen squirmed a mass of puppies, tan and black, motherless and whimpering and crawling all over one another. It reeked of urine, and wet hills of puppy poop guarded the cage door, so that you could only open it a crack without leveling off a little summit of shit. At the sound of the latch, the puppies untangled themselves, stretched, shook, and trotted over to the door, wagging their tails as my mother wiggled through the narrow opening. Very carefully she stepped over the poop and squatted down, while the puppies fought to lick her hand, tumbling and rolling over one another like socks in a dryer. One of the puppies managed to wriggle its way into her lap, leaping clumsily to lick her chin with its velvety pink tongue.

She went gaga over it, I told my father later that night.

It turned out to be a *she*, and after much debate we named her Wally. My father wanted to name her Laika, after the Russian space dog, and I suggested Heidi, because I had just seen the Shirley Temple movie and wanted to carry on the name. My mother agreed that Heidi was a good name, and we were all set to christen the dog when suddenly she dashed over to the wall and began whining and pawing and licking it like she was possessed.

103

'There must be something living in the wall,' my father said.

'Rats,' Ellie said. 'I hear them at night. What is it, girl? You hear some rats?'

'Nonsense,' my father said. 'She just likes walls. She's got a thing for walls.'

'We could call her Wally,' my mother said.

'Wally is a boy's name,' I said. 'Wally and Beaver.'

'Nothing is written in stone,' my mother said. 'I like Wally. Hey, Wally,' she said.

The puppy suddenly stopped pawing the wall and trotted over to my mother, who took it as a sign that any debate was over.

So Wally it was, and we got her a red collar, a license, and a long red leash. In the morning while my father fixed breakfast, my mother took Wally out for a short walk. It always took a little longer than she expected, because by the time she got back my father would be rushing about saying, I really have to go, Mimi, can you finish making the girls' lunches? and my mother would say, The girls can make their own lunches, Wally's got a tick I think, and she would plop Wally in her lap and comb her fingers through the dog's fur. And Ellie and I would make our lunches while my mother tended to Wally.

Even though we were eight and ten, my mother, ever vigilant about child abductors, still insisted on walking us to school, and since Wally chewed and pooped when left alone, Wally had to come too. The dog always sensed it was more than just a quick go-out-and-do-your-duty walk, and as my mother struggled to put on the leash,

Wally was straining and prancing about and then, when my mother finally said 'Okay!' Wally charged forward, gagging and yanking my mother all the way to school, with her hollering, 'Wally HEEL!' to no avail. Things worsened when we reached the school grounds, because Wally, excited by all the children, strained forward so hard that when my mother pulled back, Wally got jerked up onto her two hind legs and pawed the air frantically, which terrified the children, not just because of her frenzy but because Wally, it turned out, came from German Shepherd stock and even at three months and even under calm circumstances had grown to resemble the vicious long-snouted police dogs we saw in movies during Safety Week.

Anyway, the children huddled as my mother kissed us goodbye and tried to drag Wally away. I felt sorry for Wally, because I knew that all she really wanted was to play, and I felt sorry for my mother, whose shoulder must have hurt from all that pulling. But I also felt sorry for myself, because nobody else had to be walked to school by an overzealous mother and a police dog. I knew this was another one of my mother's quirks, but by third grade my tolerance for these quirks was beginning to wane. I wanted to be like other kids.

Wally got to be such a nuisance that one morning the principal, Mr. Watson, met my mother at the entrance to the playground.

'Wally SIT!' my mother screamed, then straightened up and smiled her smile of war. 'Is something wrong?'

'We've had some complaints,' Mr. Watson said. 'The children are frightened. Please, leave the dog at home.'

'Oh, but I can't,' my mother said. 'The dog isn't house-trained and she'll pee all over the house and I just got new carpeting to the tune of five hundred dollars and if the school would like to reimburse me for getting it cleaned that would be fine but — ' She narrowed her eyes. 'I doubt the school has that kind of money,' she confided.

I cringed. A year ago I might have been proud when she stood up to authority, like with Nance-Rhymes-With-Dance, but at this point I simply wanted her to mind.

Mr. Watson worked his jaw. 'Why can't you leave the dog in your yard?' he asked politely.

'She digs,' my mother replied. 'Roses. Prize roses. The girls are right,' she said, 'you do look like John Kennedy.'

Mr. Watson straightened up.

'It's the eyes,' she went on. 'Definitely the eyes.'

'Still,' Mr. Watson said, 'you need to keep the dog away from the school.'

My mother frowned and patted Wally, who for some miraculous reason had chosen this moment to sit peacefully at her side. 'Well,' she said, 'I wasn't going to tell you this, but the girls have a very dangerous uncle.'

'Dangerous? How?'

'Murder. Armed robbery. He's even threatened to kidnap the girls, can you believe it?'

'Isn't he . . . in prison?'

'No,' my mother sighed. 'He got off on a

106

technicality. He's a bad egg. He's the black sheep. But you can see why I'm not comfortable letting the girls walk to school all by themselves, can't you?' She patted Wally again, and Wally came out of some reverie and suddenly stuck her nose into Mr. Watson's crotch. He tried discreetly to nudge her head away, but Wally's neck muscles went into a rigorous lock.

'You must have farted,' my mother told him. 'Wally likes the smell. My husband farts in bed all the time and the dog goes right underneath the covers and camps out, you'd think it was Chanel Number Five. Listen, I'll work on the heel command,' she promised the principal. 'I'm sure she won't frighten the children much longer.'

'You can't bring that dog on the playground,' Mr. Watson said furiously as my mother walked away. 'I won't allow it.'

'Principals are such pricks,' my mother said, kissing me goodbye and looking about for Ellie, who had long since disappeared with her group of friends. 'Be good today, honey. Study hard. Learn lots.'

'Mom?'

'What's that, sweet petuny?' she said, brushing back my bangs.

'Do I have a bad uncle I never heard about?'

'No,' my mother sighed. 'No, that was a white lie. And it didn't even do any good. Do me a favor, though?' she added, standing. 'Don't tell your father?'

Before the bell rang I went to find Ellie, who was huddling with a group of girls behind the lilac bushes, where they were passing a cigarette around. When I told her what my mother had just told Mr. Watson, she laughed harshly. 'Another story, huh, Izzy?' she said. 'What do you think it'll be tomorrow? Dad's running for President?' This produced a loud whoop from her friends. 'Nana's going to the moon? We don't have a criminal uncle, Izzy.'

'I know that,' and I fought tears as the older girls jabbered amongst themselves about my mother's shortcomings and my gullibility. I felt humiliated on all sides now. Even Ellie couldn't be trusted.

As I scuffed away, Ellie caught up with me. 'Don't tell Mom I was smoking,' she said, as soon as her friends were out of earshot.

'Maybe I will, maybe I won't.'

'Please,' Ellie begged. 'She'll kill me.'

'Maybe I will, maybe I won't.'

Later during recess I sat on a swing, dragging my toe in the dirt while my friends played four-square. This dog hadn't made our lives normal at all. I wished Wally would get hit by a car. I wished she would get bitten by a rabid raccoon. I wished she would run away and the SPCA would hold her for a day and gas her. And after wishing all that, I wondered if there really was a God, and if He was going to punish me for these bad thoughts.

As I sat there, one of the boys came over and said he'd heard my uncle was a murderer. Was it true?

'No,' I said.

'But your mother said he was.'

'My mother's a liar,' I said. 'My mother's crazy.'

'You mean she made that all up? To Mr. Watson?' This seemed to excite him, and I suddenly panicked for betraying my mother.

'No,' I said. 'She exaggerated. My uncle just tried to kill someone.'

'Over what?'

'Who knows?' I said breezily. 'Maybe he just got mad. Maybe he just didn't like the guy. Maybe the guy was asking too many questions.'

'Jeez,' the boy said. 'It's true,' he reported to his friends, who had gathered behind him. 'Did he get caught?' he asked me.

'No,' I said. 'He's on the loose.'

'From where?'

'Walla Walla,' Ellie said. She'd come up from behind, and now put her arm on my shoulder. 'Solitary confinement.'

'Jeez,' the boy said. 'Don't you get scared?'

'No,' I said. 'Our father has a good gun.' I was out of control now, but I couldn't stop myself. 'And our dog attacks on command, by the way. I say the word, and you're dead.'

The boys glanced at one another, then shrugged and walked away. My mouth was dry. It was the first time I had lied to kids my age, and even with Ellie backing me up, I was disgusted with myself. I didn't want to be here, and I didn't want to be home. I didn't want to be anywhere. I felt as wretched and doomed as an orphan. If this made-up uncle, whoever he might be, could have shown up in some old clunker of a car, circling the school, eyeing the playground, I would have run over and flagged him down. Take me away, I would have said. I don't care where, just take me anywhere else but here.

12

Wally was a bad dog, and made our lives anything but normal. She never did get house-trained; she peed in the house when she was happy, sad, excited, bored — in short, all the time. She snuck up and grabbed food off our plates. She ran away. She chewed shoes and gloves and gnawed all the piping off the sofa cushions. Some nights she barked all night long, and whenever the doorbell rang, day or night, it triggered something in her head, and she ran upstairs and barked for hours at the dust kitties under the beds.

Over the summer my mother refused to acknowledge the problem. She'd gotten us a dog, and we were all going to love it, goddamn it. So she simply kept trying to train Wally. Per instructions, she sprayed her with the vinegar bottle when she was bad and handed out bits of cheese when she was good. But one day Wally chewed up my mother's quilt — a treasured possession that Nana had sewn from the scraps of my mother's childhood dresses. That did it. Suddenly my mother switched from hot to cold, tied Wally to a tree in the yard, and ran an ad in the newspaper (because even she couldn't send Wally back to the pound). 'Shepherd-lab mix,' the ad read. 'Happy 6 mo. dog needs loving home. Current owner going overseas, must sell.' We got a lot of inquiries, but when people came to visit, they could see for themselves what kind of a dog Wally was, and they always left, politely claiming that they were looking for something with a little more Shepherd in it, or a little less energy, or blue eyes, or brown eyes. ADBW, my father would say when they left. Any Dog But Wally.

Then we got a call from a friend of a friend who had heard about Wally and her problems. He lived over on the Olympic Peninsula and offered to give Wally a warm bed, a long stretch of beach, and all the patience in the world. It seemed too good to be true, so when he offered to come get Wally the next week, my mother said that we would be glad to bring Wally to him the next day. We've been meaning to visit the Olympic Peninsula, she told him. Wasn't there a rain forest over there?

Why, yes there was.

Which meant another day trip in Ethel.

My mother had always had an unsettling devotion to this car. Ethel was a dark green Plymouth, late forties' vintage, with voluptuous fenders and shiny chrome trim and a long imposing hood. My mother had bought the car second-hand, and named it after the character on 'I Love Lucy.' Ever mistrustful of certified mechanics, she quickly learned how to change the oil and replace the spark plugs and adjust the brakes herself. My father, who drove a Buick, could only borrow Ethel, with my mother's permission; and if she had any say in the matter she'd go along and sit right beside him, barking instructions like a driver's ed teacher. Don't rev the engine. Don't lug the engine. Don't ride the clutch. Slow down. Speed it up for heaven's sake Hugh you ninny.

What she liked most was to go exploring on her own. Gas was cheap, and she would take me and Ellie on day trips to the far corners of the state — through the snowy Cascades, down into Wenatchee, over to Spokane, or up into the rolling rocky hills near the Grand Coulee dam. Never one to plan things in advance, she'd wake us on a summer morning and hustle us into the car and tell us we'd get a hot dog for lunch somewhere and please not to read in the car because she didn't want anyone getting carsick. And off we went, with no map, no itinerary, just the three of us and the wide-open road.

Whenever she drove, my mother wore her red cat's-eye sunglasses, red lipstick, and a red silk scarf tied around her head. At the start of each trip she settled herself into the driver's seat, and took the scarf from her purse, and in one fluid motion she pinched its two opposing corners, stretched it across the bias, and sent it billowing upward to land like a kind of parachute over her head. Then she lifted her chin and deftly knotted it underneath. She had this bracelet, too, that she wore only on these road trips, a costumey piece made of dozens of colored glass pipes that dangled from a copper chain. Ellie and I called it the hula skirt bracelet, and privately fought over who would inherit it.

The Plymouth was huge, especially for two girls and one ninety-five-pound woman. Ellie and I could easily lie down across the back seat, which we often did when it was dark, because sometimes my mother would miscalculate and we would be miles from home at nine in the evening. Then she would stop at a gas station and telephone our father, who would scold her for her lack of planning, and for the rest of the trip Ellie and I would lie down in the back, our bony knees raised, gazing up at the stars as we drove through the night with the warm road rumbling beneath us.

During the day we always rode up front. Here we fought, because the front seat was divided into two plump square sections, and whoever sat in the middle got the prickly frayed edges of each half sticking into her back. My mother tried to convince us that the middle seat was better, since it was right next to her, but we were not convinced. So she made us alternate every fifty miles, which meant that whoever got stuck in the middle spent most of her time scrutinizing the odometer instead of watching out the window.

There were no seat belts, and Ellie and I would ride on our knees — happy, usually, to be going somewhere we had never been before. I loved to roll down the window and stick my arm out with my hand cupped against the wind. This was dangerous, my father had warned us; we could get stung by a bee that way; but my mother let us do it, because she agreed that it felt marvelous, and that the likelihood of a bee sting was not very great.

'Your father thinks every risk is a big risk,' she told us, blowing cigarette smoke out of the corner of her mouth. 'Mr. Boring. Mr. Take A

Nap and Prune the Crabapple. You know, every time we have sex he thinks I'll get pregnant. He will never ever ever just play the odds.'

Her smoking in the car didn't bother me, even when the windows were rolled up. I liked the saturated smell. It smelled like home, like my mother's bedroom to be precise, since she often smoked late into the night and if either of us had a bad dream we were always welcome in her bed. She chain-smoked as she drove, and when we stopped for gas Ellie and I had to empty the ashtray, a dirty job for which we were each given a dime, which we spent on frosty bottles of soda from an ancient rattly machine.

We were excited about the trip to the Olympics, because that was a part of the state we'd never visited. Even my father wanted to come along. It was a clear Saturday morning in late summer, and we set off early with my mother at the wheel and my father in charge of a picnic hamper he'd packed with ham sandwiches. Ellie and I sat in back with Wally.

We were just getting onto the highway when my mother threw up her hands and shrieked, 'Oh my God, we're going to hit a hundred thousand miles on this trip!'

'Hands on the wheel, Mimi,' my father said.

'This is so exciting,' my mother said, turning back to the road. 'Most cars blow up before they reach a hundred thousand miles but not this car,' she said, patting the dashboard. 'Not this baby. She's got another fifty thousand left in her, I'd put money on it.'

'You take good care of a car, it'll last forever,' my father allowed.

'We'll celebrate today,' my mother said. 'Where do you think it'll happen? Before or after Sequim?'

'Before,' I said.

'After,' my father said.

Ellie wasn't interested in odometer readings. 'Let's see. If this car lasts another fifty thousand miles, it'll be the car I go off to college in. That'll make a stunning impression,' she said.

'Don't you sound like a teenager,' my mother remarked.

'Oh, shut up,' Ellie said.

My father turned in his seat. 'Don't talk that way to your mother, Ellie.'

'You shut up, too,' Ellie said, opening a book. She had wanted to spend the day with her friends, and when Ellie was in a bad mood, she tried to get the whole world in a bad mood with her. 'Get this stupid dog away from me.'

'Come here, Wally-girl,' I murmured, pulling the dog close to me. Wally had gotten into the garbage the night before and was farting like crazy. Every few minutes there was a fresh blast of cabbage gas. I felt sorry for the dog, who had no clue that we were going to abandon her later that day.

We headed south toward Tacoma. The August sky was blue and cloudless, the blazing cone of Mount Rainier out to dwarf the snow-tipped peaks of the Cascade Range. Even the Olympic peaks rose high and clear to the west, and I tried my best to ignore Ellie's bad mood and enjoy the ride. I'd never been to the Olympic Peninsula before, and I wanted to see these rain forests my mother was talking about, see if indeed there were parrots and monkeys and rivers full of piranhas.

'This dog could send a rocket to the moon,' my father remarked.

'Yeah, open a window,' Ellie said.

'No, don't, I have a sore throat,' my mother said. 'The smell's not that bad.'

'I'm going to suffocate,' Ellie said.

'Well you just go right ahead,' my mother replied.

We had just crossed the Narrows Bridge when my mother slapped my father on the knee. 'Hugh! Wake up! It's ninety-nine thousand, nine hundred and ninety nine! Wake up, girls!'

'I'm not asleep,' Ellie grumbled. 'I'm dead.'

'This is a big moment,' my mother said. 'Here it comes — one more mile! Oh, you're entering a new stage of life, baby,' she said. 'One more hill. Point seven!' she informed us. 'Point eight!'

One hundred thousand miles on an old car: it didn't strike me as anything to get excited about, but my mother honked the horn and rolled down her window and yelled and waved her free hand in the wind. 'Isn't this thrilling?' she demanded. 'Isn't this just the most amazing car that ever lived?'

But my mother's mood plummeted as the day wore on. Wally's new owner, this blessed man with an ocean of patience, lived outside of Sequim, and we followed his directions down a long, straight road through a tidal plain, then a

117

right-hand turn, and down another long straight road, until we reached a shack of weathered wood. Outside, the air smelled of ocean breezes and decaying fish. I don't remember much about the man except that he had a splotchy purple birthmark on his neck, which I tried not to stare at. Wally raced around the shack four or five times; she trotted with her head down along some unseen loopy path, squatted briefly, then rejoined us and sat down.

'She likes walls,' Ellie told him. 'That's why we named her Wally. Are you going to keep her name?'

The man squatted and rubbed Wally behind the ears. 'Hey Wally,' he said. 'Hey Wally girl.'

'She chews things,' my mother blurted out.

'Dogs chew,' he agreed.

'Pillows and quilts,' my mother said. 'In all honesty.' I could tell she was getting cold feet, and I hoped this sudden streak of honesty would fizzle out before the man changed his mind.

He merely said he'd like a few minutes alone with Wally, to make sure he and the dog could be buddies. My father herded us into the car, where he turned on a ball game. I watched the man play with Wally. He threw a stick. Wally sat down. The man threw another stick, trotted after it, picked it up, waved it about, and threw it again. This time Wally chased it, though she did not retrieve it but rather trotted around the yard holding it proudly between her teeth. She would learn. Such a simple game, I thought. Why hadn't we thought of that?

It is not as hard as it might seem to give away

a dog. I expected to have second thoughts, but I didn't. Wally had a good home, a place to run, an indestructible house with no pillows to chew. Most of all she had a new owner who seemed to speak her language, and I pictured them down on the floor together, barking at the walls, or howling at the moon.

My mother, however, was having a hard time. She nuzzled Wally and smoothed her ears, and whispered something, until finally my father put his hand on her shoulder. 'Time to go, Mimi,' he said gently, but my mother took it the wrong way, because she said, 'Don't be so fucking condescending, Hugh,' and she stood up and walked stiffly to the car, to the passenger's seat this time, and got in.

Nobody said anything as we drove away. I thought we'd done the right thing for Wally, but not for my mother, and I was angry at her for claiming the moment, when it should have been Wally's. Always she managed to make us feel sorry for her, when we were supposed to feel good about something else. Before we turned the corner I took one look back. Wally and her new owner were chasing each other around the yard.

At least Wally could have a normal life now.

Back in Sequim my father suggested that we get an ice cream before heading home.

'Home?' my mother said. 'Kind of a waste of gas, don't you think, to come all the way over here and not even see anything but one dumpy little town?'

'Where were you thinking of going?' my father asked.

'Well the girls would like to see the Hoh,' my mother said. 'And I've never seen a rain forest. Have you?'

My father admitted that he hadn't, but pointed out that the Hoh was probably a good five-hour drive and we'd have to turn around as soon as we got there.

'Of course we couldn't just get a motel room,' my mother said, lighting another cigarette. 'You don't have your pajamas or your shaving kit, I don't have my diaphragm, God forbid we do anything spur of the moment.'

'Mother?' said Ellie.

'What's that, peanut?'

'Shut up and quit picking on Daddy.'

My mother stubbed out her cigarette, only half-smoked, and lit another. 'That's the third time today, Ellie,' she said. 'I told my father to shut up once. You know what he did?'

'What?'

'He whipped me.'

'So whip me,' Ellie said. 'Just quit picking on Daddy.'

'I don't believe in whipping children,' my mother said. 'I got whipped enough when I was a child. My father had a leather strap and whipped me whenever I was bad. One thwack for every year. I was twelve when I told him to shut up. Figure it out. I have scars, don't I, Hugh?'

My father cleared his throat. 'Let's see just how far the Hoh is,' he said, and he began unfolding the map with one hand as he drove.

'And Nana herself just stood by and watched,' my mother said. 'Can you imagine? A mother watching her own child get beaten like that?'

'Could you just apologize, please, Ellie?' my father said.

Ellie shrugged. 'Sor-ree.'

'Oh, don't be sorry,' my mother said. 'You had every right to tell me to shut up. I nag your father, I nag him way too much and some day, you know what? Some day he's going to dump me. Aren't you, Hugh?'

'No, Mimi, I'm not going to dump you. Look, here's the Hoh,' he said, pointing on the map. 'It's a long way but if you want to go, we'll go. What's the vote?'

'Go,' Ellie said.

'Go,' I said, hopefully.

'I don't care,' my mother said.

★   ★   ★

To get to the Hoh River, where the rain forests are, you have to drive from Sequim up to Port Angeles, then inland and down, making a large 'C' around the Olympics. It would have been a good four-hour drive, but in fact we never made it past Lake Crescent.

My guess now is that my mother must have been so pre-occupied with Wally those last few weeks that she simply forgot to check the oil. This was unlike her. Usually she checked the oil herself every time we got gas. But I guess everyone forgets to check the oil once in a while. Anyway, the Plymouth died just as we were approaching Lake Crescent from the east. My father was driving, and my mother was looking

121

out the window, not saying much of anything. My father had tried to get us all involved in some car game, I Spy or I Packed My Grandmother's Trunk, but my mother's silence, her purposeful withdrawal, dampened everyone's mood. I began to think that my father should have stayed home; my mother and Ellie and I could have come by ourselves, and it would have been just another trip in Ethel, and there wouldn't have been any of this tension between my parents. My mother's dark moods always deepened when we were together as a family.

As we rounded a bend, the lake came into view. It was long and narrow, curved like its name, nestled between steep mountains. 'Oh, isn't it pretty,' my mother said, 'look, girls, look at the lake,' and we all looked out at the steely gray waters, which rocked and danced in the wind, spilling over with whitecaps and sending choppy waves splashing against the rocky shoreline. It was beautiful in a primitive way, especially with the mist gathering in the peaks above. The road was hilly, and my father was continually shifting, and it was during one downshift that the Plymouth gave out its first deep, prehistoric grinding sound.

'Jesus, Hugh, put the clutch in,' my mother said, but my father said it had nothing to do with the clutch, and he gave the car a little more gas, and the engine shrieked as though a chainsaw had just hit metal.

'Jesus, Mary and Joseph!' my mother exclaimed.

My father steered the car to the side of the road, and we rolled to a stop at the edge of a steep wooded hillside that dropped precipitously to the lake. Smoke seeped from the perimeter of the hood. My father told us to stay in the car and he and my mother got out and raised the hood.

'Car's dead,' Ellie told me.

'How do you know?'

'I just know.'

'Cool,' I said.

She looked at me and laughed. We both laughed. We liked the Plymouth, but the thought of shopping for a new car, something with bucket seats and front and rear speakers, was far more thrilling than the idea of going off to college in an antique.

Outside our father took out a handkerchief and wiped his hands while our mother stood with her back to us.

'You girls stay here with your mother,' he said, leaning in through the window. 'I'm going to hitch a ride to the nearest garage.'

'Is Ethel dead?' Ellie asked.

'No. She ran out of oil.'

'Is that serious?' Ellie asked.

'Pretty serious. You wait here with your mother,' he said again. 'I'll back as soon as I can.'

'What are you going to do?' Ellie said.

'Get a tow truck,' my father said. 'Now keep your mother company. Tell her about school. Tell her about your friends. Don't let her start talking about Nana again, or Wally. All right?'

'All right,' said Ellie.

'All right,' I said.

'And don't go anywhere else,' my father said.

'Where could we go?' Ellie asked, with pronounced rhetoric; she knew her role right now, which was to take charge. My father said something to my mother, then zipped up his jacket and went and stood by the side of the road until a car came along. He waved it down, conferred with the driver, then climbed in and they drove off and we were alone.

My mother had gone over to the edge of the embankment and was looking down through a tangle of branches and vines to the water below. We got out of the car and joined her.

'What happened?' Ellie finally asked.

'Ethel's out of oil,' she said. 'Ethel blew up.'

'Don't you check the oil all the time?'

My mother smiled at the trees.

'You mean you forgot?'

'That's right,' my mother said. 'I forgot. One hundred thousand miles,' she said, looking back at Ellie. 'She had a lot of life left in her.'

I began to get scared. 'What'll happen? Will she go to a junkyard?'

'Definitely not!' my mother exclaimed. 'Can you imagine, people taking her bumper one day, her turn signal the next? I don't think so.'

I glanced into the engine, which was still smoking, its innards black and twisted and dangerous-looking. I thought this must be a terrible day for my mother, to lose both her dog and her car in the span of two hours.

'We could get her towed back home,' I suggested. 'You could fix her yourself.'

'No, that's beyond me,' my mother said. 'I'd end up putting her on cinder blocks and waiting

124

for one of you to find a boyfriend who likes to tinker with cars. Not a good life,' she said. 'Ethel deserves better.'

I didn't know what she meant by that, but I didn't ask. Instead I went over and sat down on a rock. I wondered how far away the nearest gas station was, and how long it would take my father to get back here. I thought of his warning to Ellie and me that we keep the conversation centered on easy subjects, like school and friends, but I couldn't think of anything to say.

' . . . or maybe a Mustang,' Ellie was saying.

My mother didn't seem to hear, because she suddenly excused herself and opened the car door and sat down in the driver's seat. For a few minutes she just sat there, gripping the steering wheel with her eyes closed. Then she leaned over and began rummaging through the glove compartment, stuffing papers into her pockets.

'What's she doing?' Ellie asked nervously.

'I don't know.'

'Dad said don't leave her alone. Maybe we should get her to play Hearts.'

My mother said she wasn't in the mood.

'Rummy?' I said. 'Gin?'

'No, thanks, girls,' my mother said. 'I don't really want to play cards right now.'

'How about if we sing,' Ellie offered. 'That'll pass the time.' And without waiting for an answer, she began to sing the song 'Found A Peanut,' but it seemed inappropriate, being as it was about a kid who eats a rotten peanut and dies. Not wanting to give my mother new ideas, I started singing 'Moon River,' which my mother

125

often sang to us at bedtime. My mother leaned back and closed her eyes.

'We had some good trips in this car, didn't we, girls?' she sighed, striking a match and lighting a cigarette. 'Remember the trip to the San Juans? Remember Ethel on the ferry? Once when you were babies I drove her to Vancouver and back in one night, you were crying so much. I couldn't take it. I said to your father, You put the kids to bed tonight, if I have to be in this house and listen to that crying one minute longer I am likely to murder everyone! It's very tough being a mother with two small children,' she told us, 'home alone all day long.' She sucked the cigarette so deeply that her cheeks hollowed out and the orange glow ate its way down the tip.

'She was a good car,' my mother went on. 'Did you know you were both conceived in the back seat?'

'I thought just Izzy,' Ellie said.

'Nope,' my mother said. 'Both of you. Though I guess I'm not supposed to be telling you the stories of your conception.'

'It doesn't matter,' Ellie said. 'You've told us a hundred times before, only different versions.'

My mother sighed. 'I just can't see this car going to a junkyard,' she said. She drew once more on her cigarette, then tossed it out the window and told us to look around and get anything we wanted to keep — which, assuming as I was that the car would only be temporarily in some shop, amounted to my jacket and my Nancy Drew and that's it. I left my stash of Lik-A-Maid, my Cracker-Jack ring, even my

126

picture of John Lennon making a face. My mother got out and began tossing tools and jackets and boots and empty cans of oil into a pile on the gravel. When she was done she dusted her hands on her pants.

'Go over there and stand by that big rock,' she told us, and we obeyed. She sat down in the driver's seat, and turned the steering wheel all the way to the right, and batted the stick shift back and forth. Then she stood up and, with one hand on the steering wheel and the other on the doorframe, she braced her feet and began to push. The car was on a sandy shoulder, with the right front wheel a few feet from the edge of the drop-off, and my mother pushed and released, and pushed and released some more, and the car began to rock, a little bit forward, a little bit backward, a little more forward, a little more backward. My mother gave it a good hard push, and the ground began to give way, and clumps of dirt and rock began raining down the steep incline into the lake, and with one great final push the Plymouth slowly rolled over the embankment, snapping off branches until finally it landed upside down with a resounding crash in the rocky waters of the lake below.

After what seemed like a very long time, Ellie and I joined my mother and all three of us peered over the edge. There, far below us, the car lay overturned like a giant bug. I couldn't say anything but merely stared at a car that just that morning had reached its hundred-thousand-milestone, coasting along a highway with four people inside, four people who sat on warm, dry seats and listened to a ball game on a radio and looked through unbroken windows to see the sights along their journey; and all I could think was that my mother was crazier than I knew.

For a long time, nobody said anything. Finally my mother looked at us with a queer smile that sank a stone into the pit of my stomach. 'Haven't you always wanted to do something like that?' she said, nudging me. 'Truthfully? Haven't you?'

No, I thought. I have never had the urge to push a car over the edge of a cliff into a lake.

'Do you think I can convince your father that she rolled off by herself?'

'No,' I said.

'Oh Izzy,' my mother said, 'you're right, of course. I shouldn't lie about it, should I? You're my conscience, Izzy. You're my moral compass.'

I felt dizzy, then, and went to sit down on the same rock where Ellie and I had been sitting right before my mother pushed the Plymouth over the edge. If I was my mother's moral compass, then I had failed to show her the way.

Just then a tow truck crested the hill; it slowed down and pulled over to where we were standing. My father opened the passenger door and stepped out, looking around.

'She's in the lake,' my mother said before he could even ask. 'Oh Hugh, Ethel was dead. I didn't want her to go to some junkyard.'

'The lake?'

'I pushed her in, Hugh,' my mother said with a shrug. 'I gave her a proper burial.'

'You pushed her? You pushed the car into the lake?'

128

'Why, she rolled right over the edge!' my mother exclaimed, as though both proud of and surprised by her strength. 'She wasn't heavy at all!'

My father went to the edge of the hillside and looked down. 'You sank the car,' he said. 'Are you telling me you sank the car? Is she telling the truth?' he asked Ellie and me.

We nodded.

He looked at my mother in disbelief, and stared down at the car again. He was speechless. We all were.

I think the tow truck man prevented my father from committing an act of violence that afternoon, because at that moment he stepped forward and looked down at the car and whistled. 'You did that?'

'Yes I did,' my mother said proudly.

The man put his hands on his hips, and looked from my father to Ellie and me again, and suddenly he tipped his head back and burst out laughing. He laughed so hard that finally he had to take his handkerchief out and wipe his eyes, and in the meantime my mother grinned broadly, and finally my father, who'd been staring at the ground, managed a little wheeze. I laughed too, but only out of relief that the grownups were laughing. Truth be told, I was way too young to understand the concept of absurdity, and didn't see anything funny in the situation at all.

The scene ended with dignity: finally we all squeezed into the tow truck and the man drove us to the lodge at the west end of the lake, where he dropped off my mother and Ellie and me, while he and my father went to get a bigger tow truck with the capacity to haul the car up out of the water. We spent the rest of the afternoon playing board games in a sunroom overlooking the lake. My father came back just before dinner, his hands scratched, his shirt torn. My mother didn't ask a single question about the car, and, on cue, neither did we. That night we ate lamb chops in the restaurant, and blackberry cobbler, and Ellie and I slept in a room of our own and kept the windows open, listening to the water lap against the shoreline.

The next morning, after breakfast, Ellie and I walked down to the pebbly shoreline and threw stones into the water. I asked Ellie what it all meant, our mother pushing a car into the lake. She was crazy, wasn't she? We already knew that, Ellie said. Did it mean she was going to go away to a hospital again? I asked, and Ellie said she didn't know. I asked if this was a sign that she was going to try and take a lot of pills again. Ellie looked at me and said, Maybe, and I began to cry, because no matter how much I might have hated my mother back on the side of the road, she was still my mother, and always would be, and I would be totally and utterly lost without her, no matter how crazy she was. I was scared, standing on the beach with Ellie. All along I had thought that my mother's visits with the doctor were helping her, that she was getting better, that every day she didn't kill herself meant she was walking away from the dark and toward the light. Now I knew that every day she didn't kill herself meant only one thing — that she hadn't killed herself that particular day. It could always happen the next day, or the day after that, or the day after that. We were never home safe.

After a while our father joined us. He skipped a few stones, then stood with his arms around our shoulders, wondering out loud how Wally's first night with her new owner had gone. I'd forgotten all about Wally, and I grabbed onto the thought of that dog like a life jacket. Wally, the solution to all our problems. The dog who was going to make our family normal.

Standing there as a threesome, we heard a loon out on the lake, but the overall silence was broken by the sound of my mother's voice. Time to go home, she called from the porch above, and for a minute I felt as though we'd simply come as a family for a nice weekend getaway. Come on up, my mother called. We've got things to do.

13

The more you prod my sister Ellie, the more she holds back. Ask if she's happy with her psychiatrist, and she'll tell you how much he charges. Try to find out if she's on the right medication, and she'll marvel over her friend who's the model case, takes twenty milligrams of Prozac day after day, year after year and does just fine. Talk about the news, though, or dilly-dally on about some tedious case you have, and pretty soon she'll be telling you everything you want to know.

I see this happening in the bathroom. All she'll say for the moment is that she's fine with the idea of a divorce. I leave her and join the group upstairs, where it seems that Rachel has been showing everyone how well she can read, to which end she has opened up the front page of the newspaper, where there is a full-color picture of two grinning children riding the roller coaster at the carnival. In the caption below, Rachel has artfully deciphered the words 'this weekend.'

What little resistance she gets dissipates completely when she produces a few crumpled dollar bills from her pocket and asks if this would be enough to get us into the carnival? Because she would be willing to pay for us all? If we'd just take her? Please?

My father checks his watch. 'What about dinner plans?'

'I thought we'd go out,' Gabe says.

My father looks worried. 'I hope you made reservations,' he says. 'I don't know about you people, but if I have to wait more than fifteen minutes I end up having too darn much wine, and then I don't care what the heck I'm eating, it might as well be a hamburger.'

'We're all set,' Gabe says, and without looking at me he flees the room. I hear the door to my study close, and inwardly smile at the thought of him madly flipping through the phone book for a good restaurant.

'So can we go?' Rachel asks.

'Go where?' says Ellie. She has silently rejoined us, looking slick and dewy from the shower, dressed now in a long rumpled linen shift, with armholes you could fit your head through. Thankfully, she has covered herself underneath with a lacy black camisole. Rachel shows Ellie the newspaper and tells her the plans. At first Ellie says no, because she gets overwhelmed by crowds, but Rachel starts to whine about how they never get to do this kind of thing in New York, it's always the zoos and museums and if Dad were here he'd say yes.

I wonder if I am the only one who thinks that kids lose their charm when their parents show up.

Ellie cups Rachel's chin and brushes a few corkscrews off the girl's forehead. 'You're right,' she says. 'We never do things like this. Though I want you to understand that whether Dad would say yes is beside the point.'

'So we're going?'

133

'Promise to behave?'

'Promise!'

'Tell me if this is something Wilson can brag about,' Ellie declares as I lock up the house. 'Small town festival, good family fun? Not his specialty, believe me. So go right ahead, you tell me who's got the child's best interests at heart.'

'I didn't know it was an issue.'

'It's not,' Ellie says darkly, 'not yet. But,' she adds, 'that doesn't mean I can't make it an issue, does it, my dear? Did you check the stove?'

I cast her a sharp look. This is a direct reference to our mother, who without fail checked the stove, the iron, the furnace, and the hot water heater — checked each of them several times, in fact — whenever she left the house.

Ellie gives me a playful shove. 'Just a joke,' she says. 'I'm not kidding, Izzy, you're too fucking serious these days.'

★ ★ ★

After a heated debate, we manage to persuade Ellie to let Rachel ride with Gabe and me in our Subaru station wagon while Ellie rides with our father in the Land Cruiser. Ellie was fine with the idea until she saw that Gabe had to flip over the back seat to dislodge the seat belts, which in their twisted, matted state offered little visual reassurance.

'Hmm,' she began, 'maybe,' but my father stepped in.

'Look,' he declared, and he folded himself into the back seat. He buckled the seat belt and threw his body forward. 'The seat belts are fine, Ellie. Rachel will be fine. Let her go.' In response to which Ellie froze up in deep silence, no doubt weighing everyone's responsibilities, until my father simply went ahead and guided Rachel into the back seat of the Subaru and buckled her snugly and nodded for Gabe and me to go before Ellie found something else to worry about.

This scene, minor as it should have been, disturbed me. Here was my sister, still worrying the little issues to death. She has always done this, even as a child. Once she became obsessed with finding an overdue library book while our mother was up in the attic with a gas mask on, spraying Raid into the rafters. Now, thirty years later, she's worrying about seat belts when Rachel's entire world is about to come crashing down on her with the divorce.

Gabe starts the engine and the three of us drive down the mountain. It is nice to have a child in the back seat of our car. If one of those Clomid injections had worked, our own child could be sitting back there with Rachel. A little girl with bangs and chubby knees. Or a chunky boy with large seashell ears. I try not to dwell.

'Look, a deer!' exclaims Rachel. A young buck grazes on the side of the road, while a doe lies in the shade of an apple tree.

'Did you get dinner reservations?' I ask Gabe.

'Not yet.'

'What are we going to do?'

'I don't know.'

'My father makes big deals out of birthday

dinners,' I warn him.

'Don't bug me,' he says. 'I'll keep calling.'

I figure I should wait until we are alone to tell him about the state of my sister's marriage, but I can't help fishing for a little more information from Rachel.

'When are you going to France, Rachel?'

'We're not going this year,' she says, scanning the forest for more deer.

'Your dad's over there now?'

'Yup.'

'Miss him?'

She just shrugs, so I switch subjects. 'Is your mom painting a lot these days?'

'She's doing my portrait,' Rachel says. 'I only have half a face, but she says it's supposed to be that way.'

'Your mom's a really good painter, isn't she?'

'Yes,' Rachel says. 'She likes blue the most.'

Gabe murmurs something about black.

'And I look kind of sad in the picture,' says Rachel. 'I wish she'd make me smile. Do you know what's really sad?'

'No, what?'

'My parents are getting divorced.'

Gabe taps the brakes.

'I heard,' I tell her.

'Mom says Dad may not even be able to come back to New York at all, like ever, because of taxes,' Rachel volunteers. 'But if he can't come back, I get to go to a school in Switzerland.'

'Would you like that?'

'Only if my mother can live with me,' Rachel says. 'I get real homesick for her.'

'You do?'

'And she says she's paid every cent of her taxes, so we could come home if we wanted. What are taxes, anyway? Oh look!' she exclaims. 'There's the roller coaster!'

We have arrived at the town's central park, a few shady acres with a mountain-fed creek running through it, a creek which in spring roars down through the canyon but at this time of year is so low that children wade freely in its rocky pools. In the center of the park, a large white tent has been erected for the weekend, with music and folk dancing inside. But most of the crowd is outside, strolling walkways lined for the weekend with ice cream carts, falafel stands and sausage grills sending off their plumes of smoke. Craft booths flutter with silky scarves and tie-dyed shirts, children squat to get their faces painted, dogs sniff for discards, and shirtless young men toss colored wands spinning high into the air.

'It's not very big,' Rachel says of the roller coaster.

She's right, the roller coaster rises no higher than a parent's head. What interests her far more is a giant yellow inflated castle with twenty or so kids inside, all of them jumping and toppling and lurching about like little drunks. My father buys a packet of tickets, Ellie counts out the requisite number, and Rachel runs off to join the fun. Gabe and my father wander over to a kayaking booth, while Ellie and I sit down on a nearby bench.

When she is sure our father is out of sight,

Ellie takes out a pack of cigarettes and lights one.

'Here's where we really missed out,' she says, cupping her hand against her side in case our father should reappear. 'Remember the World's Fair and how Dad wanted to take us to the Seattle Center and Mom said no?'

Carnivals and fairs were off limits when we were growing up because, according to our mother, the food would have salmonella, or the Ferris wheel would crack, or someone just out of the state penitentiary would snatch us from the crowd and whisk us off to Mexico, or Istanbul.

'Look at her,' Ellie says, watching Rachel bounce and tumble in the castle. 'Is she having a total blast or what? I hate to brag but I think I'm a pretty damn good mother, don't you?'

'What's up with Wilson's taxes? And I thought you quit.'

Ellie drops her cigarette and grinds it into the grass with her toe, an act for which I fear the wrath of the city at large. We don't do that in this town.

'I don't know anything about his taxes,' she says. 'I keep out of it. Especially now that we're splitting up. What I don't know won't hurt me.'

'That's not quite true,' and I am about to explain the concept of joint liability to her, when I happen to glance over at the kayak display. My father has put on a helmet, and is climbing into a yellow kayak that lies tilted on the grass.

Ellie goes on, 'What are they going to do, lock us both up?'

'Have they brought charges?'

'No, they just send him threatening letters. Wilson's not the most organized guy on this planet, you know. He can never find the documents he needs. Anyway, his girlfriend will bail him out if push comes to shove.'

'So there's a girlfriend.'

'Hey, not just any girlfriend — an Italian heiress! Who of course has nothing to do with the reason we're splitting up. Hey, sweetie pie!' she exclaims as Rachel runs toward us. 'Was it fun? Do you want to go again?'

Rachel has another girl with her. 'This is Marta,' she says. 'Marta lives here.' Marta smiles at us and I take an instant dislike to her. It's not because she's wearing a South Park T-shirt, or because her hair has been sectioned into dozens of tiny beaded braids that probably cost a fortune. It's her Eddie Haskell smile, phony and practiced and wicked as a snake.

'Just one more time,' Ellie warns Rachel. The girls dash back to the castle as a cloud darkens the sky.

I take off my sunglasses. 'How long has this been going on?'

'Ever since we stopped having sex,' Ellie says. 'It's fine with me, though. Wilson gets laid and I get a bank account and Rachel gets whatever she needs. From me, anyway. She certainly could use a little more attention from her father.'

'I thought he took her on trips, and helped out at the school.'

'All for show,' Ellie says. 'Only if people are watching, so he can rack up the Good Dad points. Otherwise he spends his time having lunch with Big Very Important People, ironing out deals. Fuck, it gets cold quickly here,' she says, drawing her arms around her. 'Where'd the sun go?'

'Deals for what?'

'Don't ask, Izzy,' Ellie says wearily. 'What you don't know won't hurt you.' She stands up and wanders over to a jewelry booth, drawn to its display of silver necklaces on a black velvet board. She fingers a shimmering rope of liquid silver, with tiny bits of lapis. The man tending the booth watches silently. He is wearing mirrored sunglasses which, along with the droopy mustache and bushy sideburns, make him look like he dropped into the wrong decade.

'You want to try it on?' he asks my sister, and without waiting he lifts the necklace and fastens it around her neck. She does not move away as he bends close. When he stands back and hands her a mirror, she opts instead to look into his sunglasses.

'You definitely have the neck,' he tells her, gazing back. 'That's what I told myself when I made this piece, I told myself it's definitely gotta have a very long neck.'

Ellie turns her head slightly, but keeps staring into his glasses. 'What do you think, Izzy?'

'It's gorgeous,' I say.

'How much?' Ellie asks.

'Three twenty,' he says.

Ellie tilts her head the other way. She looks like Audrey Hepburn to me, with her long bare neck. The sky darkens further, and the man

140

removes his sunglasses. He has one blue eye and one brown eye. Parents used LSD, that's my guess.

'Where are you from?' he asks.

'Oh, California,' my sister replies absently, and when he asks why she is here in town, she tells him she's giving a paper at a conference on biogenetics.

'Got a black dress?'

'Why, yes, come to think of it,' Ellie says, 'as a matter of fact, I do have a black dress.'

'Then you're set.'

'What do you think, Izzy,' she says to me. 'Too sexy for a conference?'

It sure is, especially with a black dress, but I shrug. I can't believe she's going to drop three-hundred and twenty dollars on a necklace for herself. Then again, she's rich and I'm not.

'Okay,' she says, 'I'll take it.' As the man wraps the necklace in tissue, my sister opens her wallet and counts out four hundred-dollar bills. Taking the money, the man hands her his business card. 'In case you ladies need anything else,' he explains.

'Jesus, and I thought I was a good liar,' I remark as we walk back toward the castle.

Ellie shrugs. 'Assholes never deserve the truth.'

'Why was he an asshole?'

'He came on to me.'

'He did? And what are you doing, carrying around that much cash?'

'Isabella, are you always so prudent?' she asks wearily. She hands me the bag with the necklace. 'Happy birthday. What?' she demands. 'You

141

think I go around dropping this much money on myself just because I'm rich? A little more credit please?'

'God,' I say, catching my breath, 'thank you. It's beautiful.'

'Yeah, well don't get gooshy, it's just a necklace.'

The yellow castle is still rocking with children. 'Where's Rachel?' I ask.

Ellie squints, even though the sun is still behind a cloud. Neither of us sees anyone with curly red hair in a Pepto-Bismol T-shirt.

'This always happens,' she says. 'She disappears on me and then pops up in my face. Drives me nuts. Put the necklace on. I want to see how it looks.'

I fasten the necklace around my neck. Instantly the silver warms to my skin.

'That's the good thing about having a kid with red hair,' Ellie says, 'they always stick out in a crowd. She's here, somewhere,' she says, gazing around.

14

Not until she has twice circled the castle does Ellie realize that Rachel has in fact disappeared — at which point panic washes over her face, and she breaks into a clumsy run. Her screams are hoarse and gravelly, the kind that make people look up with concern. This is no frazzled mother simply calling a wayward child for the fifth time. Mothers wheel their strollers aside and fathers pause with toddlers on their shoulders, asking for a description. I tell them what Rachel looks like and what she's wearing as Ellie beelines over to the creek, stumbling and splashing into the water. 'Rachel!' she yells, hitching up her jumper. 'Rachel!'

'What's up?' Gabe asks, right in my ear so that I jump a little.

'Shit, don't do that. We can't find Rachel. Where's my father?'

'Still over by the kayaks.'

'Ellie!' I shout, and my sister turns, knee-deep in the stream. 'Go check out the kayaks!' She looks where I am pointing, then stumbles through the water toward the shallow pool, where people in kayaks bob about like colorful bath toys.

'Anyone check out the tent?' Gabe asks, and when I tell him no, he heads off in that direction. I continue to scan the crowd, a little scared but mostly annoyed: wherever my sister goes, drama must follow.

Any minute Rachel will show up, I tell myself.

Ellie comes back from the kayak display out of breath. Her face is blotchy-white, like a fruit that's just been peeled. We both spy a policeman ambling in our direction, a slightly overweight young man in need of sunscreen and a few quarts of lemonade. Ellie grabs his arm and barks out the facts, adding that Rachel is about to join the ranks of the faces on the milk cartons; that every second counts, that if we wait any longer the kidnapper will be halfway to Kansas City with a fifty-pound girl bound and gagged in the back seat.

The policeman listens with his head bowed. 'Okay,' he says, looking around. 'Okay.'

'Excuse me but no, it's not okay,' Ellie retorts. 'You got a missing child, you don't just stand there.'

'First things first,' he begins.

'No, not first things first, you idiot! Go barricade the festival and then we can talk about first things first! Go on!' she says, waving her arm. 'Set up a line!'

I glance away, remembering a time long ago when Ellie herself got lost in the Seattle Public Library. With a swift and decisive manner I'd never witnessed before, my mother ordered the librarians to lock the doors and announced over the intercom that nobody was leaving until she got her daughter back. As it turned out, Ellie had merely wandered off to the water fountain. My mother, who could have looked quite foolish,

144

simply told everyone they were free to leave and led Ellie and me to the children's room, where she read us fairy tales for the next hour as though nothing had happened.

Perturbed by the heat, his sunburn, and being called an idiot, the policeman takes out his radio and requests a backup. He asks Ellie how long Rachel has been gone. Ten minutes at least, she says. The policeman asks if she has checked with Missing Children. She says by the time she finds the fucking Missing Children booth, Rachel will be not just missing but dead.

Then she squats down and rocks back and forth. 'Oh my God, if anything has happened to her I will kill myself.'

At that point, another policeman pedals up on a bicycle. He's dressed in dark gray shorts and shirt, and wears thin wraparound sunglasses.

'We have a lost child,' the first policeman explains.

Ellie stands up. 'She's missing, not lost, and Jimmy Stewart here doesn't want to do anything about it. Hey, never mind, go find some cars to ticket. Nice job you guys are doing,' she remarks. 'No wonder you can't figure out who killed JonBenét.'

'Ellie, stop it,' I tell her. 'It's her only child,' I explain to the policemen.

'What does she look like?' the bicycle cop asks.

'Red hair,' I say, 'and she's wearing a pink T-shirt.'

'Have you checked with Missing Children?'

'Yes, sir,' says Gabe, who has just returned. 'No luck. I couldn't find your dad, either,' he tells me. 'I swear, they were together.'

'How old is the grandfather?' asks the first cop.

'Hey, now that's something to really focus on, a seventy-one-year-old man,' says Ellie. 'Come on, what's it gonna take to get you moving? You need a little cash? Here, I've got cash, I've got lots of cash. What are you waiting for?'

The bicycle cop removes his glasses. His eyes are pale blue, the color of ice caves. 'We don't need cash, ma'am, but a little respect would go a long way.' Ellie crosses her arms and looks away. 'What's the child's name?' he asks me.

'Rachel.'

'And how old is she?'

'What, you want to know if she's got boobs yet too?' says Ellie.

'Shut up, Ellie. She's seven,' I tell the policeman.

Just then the radio spits static. The first policeman walks off, and I hear something about the roller coaster. I crane my neck over the crowd.

'We're trying to help,' the blue-eyed policeman is telling Ellie. 'You're not making it easy.'

'Yeah, well, I don't know about you but when I lose a child I don't consider it my job to make things easy for people,' says Ellie. She glances in the direction of the kiddie rides. A fire truck has pulled up and now its lights begin flashing. Meanwhile the first policeman has returned, and when he tells us there has been an accident on the roller coaster, all of us know Rachel is involved. Ellie breaks into a knock-kneed run,

146

and we all follow, and over the general din of the summer festival I can hear my mother warning us, once again, that Ferris wheels and small-town roller coasters can never be trusted.

★　★　★

I used to lie in bed with her and trace the burns on her arm, playing dot to dot. She told me they were grease burns. She said when she was sixteen she'd been helping Nana fry donuts, and Nana had spilled water into the black cauldron, and the hot fat spattered all over my mother's arm. Nana put butter on it, she told me. Youch.

One night I walked unnoticed into her bedroom and saw her stubbing out a half-smoked cigarette on her arm. I heard the hiss and smelled the singed hair, the burnt flesh. She looked up and her face turned pink. Youch, she said.

★　★　★

According to the man who runs the roller coaster, Rachel and Marta were standing up and he shouted for them to sit down and they didn't, and then Rachel looked back and lost her balance and fell out of the car. He thinks she fell all of five, maybe six feet.

According to Rachel, Marta made her stand up.

According to Marta, Rachel claimed you were supposed to ride the roller coaster that way.

And according to the straw-hatted woman

who has been kneeling and holding Rachel's head until Ellie arrives, the two girls were way out of control. What were they doing, riding the roller coaster without any supervision?

At least Rachel is talking. A small gash above her eye has produced an alarming amount of blood, but her vital signs — her ability to howl and writhe when the paramedic holds her wrist and tries to take a pulse — these vital signs assure us that the injuries are not life-threatening. The paramedic unwraps a lollipop and sticks it in Rachel's mouth. Rachel sucks, and grows quiet.

Ellie, who has nudged the straw-hatted woman aside, bows over Rachel, yoga-like. When the paramedic suggests she take Rachel to the emergency room, Ellie nods mutely.

'I think the girl's going to be fine,' the paramedic says, 'but since she's had a head trauma, I'd get her checked out.'

Ellie smoothes Rachel's hair back.

'Come on,' I tell her. 'I'll take you over to the hospital.'

'What about Dad?'

'Gabe'll find him,' I say. 'We'll meet up back at the house.'

Ellie helps Rachel stand. She hoists the child up against her chest, lacing her fingers beneath Rachel's bottom. Rachel relaxes. With her head limp against her mother's shoulder and her thin legs dangling against Ellie's hips, she reminds me of a floppy sock-monkey.

'I'm sorry about this,' Ellie says as we walk toward the car.

'Sorry for what?'

'Ruining your birthday,' Ellie says.

'Oh for Pete's sake,' I say. 'For Pete's sake, Ellie.'

To my surprise the emergency room is not crowded, and we get seen within an hour. The doctor peers into Rachel's eyes and taps her knees and runs his finger up the soles of her bare feet. He ends up placing two stitches in the cut above her eye, which terrifies both Rachel and Ellie, but within half an hour we are dismissed with a sheet of instructions and a few cautionary words to Rachel about not standing up in roller coasters.

'What a day,' I say, driving home.

Ellie lights a cigarette and cracks the window. 'I was never really very worried,' she says. I glance at her. 'It's just that your mind plays games,' she says. 'You come up with these worst-case scenarios. Mom was pretty good at that, wasn't she?'

I allow a faint smile.

'But you just have to tell yourself, whoa, girl, don't go down that road.' She turns around. 'How're you doing, snuggle-bunny?'

'Good,' says Rachel.

Ellie reaches back and finger-combs Rachel's hair. 'It's a wonder I keep my sanity, raising you.'

We have just started up the mountain when a raindrop spatters rudely on the windshield. Then another, followed by another, and within seconds a sheet of rain slaps down upon us. I slow the car as bubbles dance furiously on the road ahead. Quickly it turns to hail, and the hammering is so loud that no one can be heard, the windshield wipers won't go fast enough and finally I have to pull over, at which point Rachel without permission opens her door, gets slammed with a gust of BB's, yanks her little body back inside and closes the door to watch the storm from behind the safety of the window.

'If Mom were here she'd be out dancing,' Ellie remarks.

'Oh yeah! Tell me that story again,' Rachel says. 'How she went out dancing in the rain.'

'Not now, sweetheart.'

Then, as quickly as it began, the storm is over. Gently I ease back onto the road. The tires crunch on the hail. Nobody speaks. A queer light has settled over the hills, making everything seem at once close up and far away. It is six-thirty, I note, and the evening ahead suddenly seems very long, and anticlimactic.

I flash back on a summer night long ago, a very different sort of night, one that was not long at all, or anticlimactic. I can't tell if it happened, or if I'm just imagining it, but I am alone with my mother in the front seat of the Plymouth. It's just the two of us and we're cruising through golden wheat fields on our way to Montana. We have a big bag of cheese popcorn and cold bottles of Coca-Cola. My mother has rolled down the window and is singing Beatles' songs along with the radio. *If I fell in love with you, would you promise to be true?* Simple songs, simple problems. *And help me understand.*

15

My mother was the lying star of the world, and not just about exotic terminal illnesses, or criminal uncles prowling the school play-ground. She'd earned her college degree in botany, which laid the foundation for a slew of possibilities, and at any one time she might be telling people she was researching an antidote to poisonous mushrooms, or cataloguing pine beetle damage. She had an extensive botanical vocabulary and the only time she got caught was when she ran into a professor of biology from the University of Washington at my sixth-grade band concert. She knew then to shut up.

And it was funny, because as her daughters, Ellie and I were sometimes so completely taken in that we actually believed that while we were off at school, our mother was indeed out gathering specimens. Maybe she did have a lab somewhere, maybe our money had come from the National Institutes of Health. You believe what you want to believe about your parents, and from personal experience I can say that the older you get and the crazier they get, the more gullible you let yourself be, just to survive.

But in truth there was also a lot we couldn't ignore, no matter how much we wanted to think of our mother as a Nobel scientist. When she found a dead mouse in the washing machine, she became convinced that its germs were indestructible, which meant she couldn't use the washing machine again, which in turn meant she had to lug everything up to the laundromat, no small task with two pre-teen daughters and a husband who needed a freshly laundered shirt every day. When a friend of mine got lice, my mother, afraid the vermin might hunker down in strange places, plucked out her eyebrows and burned our bedding. Easy precautions to take, she claimed, when you thought of the consequences. Besides, she asked my father, what was the big deal? You of all people know about precautions, hmmm? Mr. Take Them All The Time?

Then she found a spider nest in the laundry hamper, and became convinced that the house was infested with black widows. Any normal mother would have told herself that, first, black widows didn't live in Seattle; second, even if they did, a house would not be infested; and third, even if you got bitten, it didn't mean you were going to die.

Not my mother. Convinced of the infestation, she emptied the cupboards and closets and vacuumed every square inch of the house — having first doused the vacuum bag with Raid so the spiders couldn't crawl back out. Then she fumigated the house with some chemical she got from a mail order supply. Only after spraying did she read the list of toxic compounds on the can, which convinced her we would all get cancer if we stayed in the house — and so, against my father's objections, she checked us into a motel for a week, where we could shower as many times as she told us to. Even after that week her original fear lingered. Every night she checked under our beds with a flashlight and put on fresh sheets and snuck in a few sprays with the can of Raid when she thought we weren't looking.

Because, she said to our father, you can never be too sure.

Oddly, whenever Nana came to visit, my mother was able to control her behavior. She took off her head scarf and packed away all the cans of Raid and used the washing machine and let my father's little dots of pee dry up on the toilet rim. She let us drink water from the tap and milk straight from the carton. She let us eat hamburgers. She kissed us. It amazed me, how she could simply switch off the craziness. Of course as soon as Nana left, it started all over again. My father got a cold sore and my mother made him wear a mask and nobody kissed anybody for the next month. She bought three cases of Raid, on sale. She found a lump in her breast, which turned out to be her rib bone, which humiliated her.

Ellie's reaction at that point was to ignore my mother. Maybe it had to do with being thirteen, but she got up in the morning and went off to school before my mother even woke up, and after school she studied in the library, or went over to a friend's house to listen to records. Finally around six o'clock she came home, only to eat dinner as quickly as possible and then disappear to our bedroom. I figure she probably spent all of twenty minutes every twenty-four hours in my mother's presence, those days.

153

As for me, I always felt compelled to help my mother. I thought that if I made life easier for her, she would calm down and stop plucking out her eyebrows and maybe cook a normal dinner once in a while. One day I volunteered to take the laundry up to the laundromat.

'You've got homework to do, Izzy sweetheart,' my mother chirped. 'Besides, the laundromat is full of some very, very strange people.'

I don't think she trusted me. That, or she couldn't bear to reveal that she added rat poison to the rinse cycle.

I can remember a time, probably near the end, when I decided that what my mother needed was for someone to just go ahead and run a load through our washing machine and prove to her that we wouldn't all drop dead from year-old mouse germs. One Saturday morning — I would have been eleven, maybe twelve — I got up early and collected a load of whites and tiptoed down into the basement. There beneath a mud-spattered window stood the washing machine with its lid open, waiting. I stuffed the clothes in and turned on the water and poured in the soap, but I had forgotten how much noise our machine made, and it wasn't long before I heard footsteps on the stairs and turned to see my mother, standing halfway down in her white nightgown, one hand gripping the railing. In a barely audible voice she asked me what I was doing.

Laundry, I said.

Please come upstairs, she said.

Look, I said, our washing machine's fine.

154

Come upstairs, Izzy, she said. For all its diminution, her voice had a military effect, and I obeyed.

Upstairs in the kitchen she made me scrub my hands with Comet and soak my feet in hydrogen peroxide. Swishing the water around my ankles, she said she appreciated my help but she had her own system and really, I should leave it to her. I suggested that maybe her system was too much work, and maybe she should just let me do the laundry, right here at home, normally. She said there was a lot that I didn't understand, and never would. I said, Try me. But she merely brushed the hair off my forehead and didn't answer.

Later that morning my father drew me aside and said that what I had done was brave and courageous, but he didn't think it should fall upon my shoulders to help my mother change her ways. I told him he was wrong. If not me, who else? He certainly wasn't doing anything about it, I said.

By the time Ellie woke up, my mother had already gone up to the laundromat to re-wash the load of whites I'd contaminated. As my sister poured herself a bowl of Frosted Flakes, I told her what I'd done, and Ellie, who was prone these days to ignoring most everything I said, stopped eating and gazed at me with the kind of admiration I'd always yearned for. 'I never would have dared to do that,' she said.

'One of us has to,' I said.

'Has to what?'

'Take care of her. Get her to stop.'

'Why?' Ellie said crossly. 'Why can't she fix things herself?'

I didn't have an answer for that.

'She makes us be a mother to her,' Ellie went on. 'Why can't she be a mother to us for once? I swear, if I ever decide to have kids, I'm going to grow up first.'

'Dad's grown up,' I pointed out. I felt bad about what I'd said to my father earlier, about not doing anything.

'Hah! Dad's terrified.'

A sick feeling washed over me. Grown men weren't supposed to be scared. But Ellie was right, our father was scared. Who wouldn't be, trying to raise two kids and keep his wife from swallowing a bunch of pills? Nightmares always lurked in the closet for him. No wonder he took precautions all the time.

That morning, I wanted Ellie to come up with a plan. I wanted her to say, Okay, that was a good first step and here's what we do now, we throw away the rubber gloves and the Raid and take her by the hand and wash the clothes in the washing machine and dry them and wear them. We show her the world doesn't end if we do this. We tell her we know she doesn't have a lab, we know she's not studying pine beetles, we know all about her and that's okay — all she has to do is be our mother.

If Ellie could just say something like that.

Instead, Ellie gave a shrug and put her cereal bowl in the sink and went upstairs to take a shower. But when I look back on it, I can see that Ellie had her own ways of taking charge. She never challenged our mother head-on, but on the bad nights, when my mother shut herself in her room, it was Ellie who fixed dinner and set the table and made sure there were no cigarettes smoldering in the sofa cushions. It was Ellie who went about the house with a shopping bag, gathering up my mother's odd collections of Listerine bottles and Band-Aid tins, stacking up newspapers and throwing out all the old magazines. When my father was out of town taking depositions, it was Ellie who checked the doors at night and turned off all the lights.

Just when we thought things could get no worse, my mother would wake up some morning with a wide-eyed, astonished look, as though she couldn't believe her luck. She'd bounce out of bed and get herself dressed and make our lunches and send us off to school with blowsy kisses. She'd start cooking again, real food, not a cold poached salmon that would last a week but noodley casseroles and breads and cookies and pies and cakes. She combed her hair and let her eyebrows grow back and stopped burning herself with cigarettes, and when my father got home in the evening she'd have a pitcher of martinis waiting and they would sit and cuddle and watch the news together. After dinner she played the piano, loud pieces in 4/4 time with lots of wooden chords, songs she must have plucked from the very farthest corners of her memory. I felt ecstatic, greedy, and terrified all at once.

One day, Ellie and I came home from school to find her curled up on the guest room bed, reading a magazine. The window was open and a bowl of cherries was nestled in the crook of her waist. 'Oh, girls, come and talk!' she called out as we headed for our room.

'We've got homework,' Ellie said, but my mother patted the nubby white spread and scooched over to make room. 'Come on in and talk to me, girls,' she said. 'Tell me things — I've missed so much! Tell me everything.' I looked at Ellie, and we cautiously went in and sat down on the guest room bed with her. The ruffled curtains swelled and the bedspread felt warm where my mother had been.

Nobody knew what to say.

'Well?' and my mother waited. 'Okay, then,' she said, 'I'll ask the first question. What do you want to be when you grow up?'

'I don't know,' I said.

'Me neither,' said Ellie.

'Good!' my mother exclaimed, slapping the bedspread hard enough to send dust shimmering in the air. 'You shouldn't know at your age. Now it's your turn. Ask me what I'm going to be when I grow up!'

'You're already grown up,' Ellie pointed out.

My mother gave her a playful nudge. 'I knew you'd say that,' she said. 'But I only look grown up. I'd like to be something really different, you know? Like maybe a trick rider in a circus. Or maybe I could work with baboons in Africa, like that Jane Goodall person.'

'I'd like to do that,' I said eagerly. 'We just read about her in school. Only it's chimps, not baboons.'

'Wouldn't that be something?' my mother said

dreamily. 'Living in the jungle all by yourself, taking notes and eating berries and learning chimp language? I'll bet Jane Goodall is the happiest woman on earth.'

And for a moment I entertained the notion of my mother and me going off to Africa to study chimpanzees with Jane Goodall. I saw us driving a Jeep through the jungle, both of us outfitted in shorts and boots and hats to protect us from the equatorial sun. My mother would take lots of pictures. I would write books. We would become a famous team, and win many prizes.

'Dad's home,' Ellie announced with a note of relief in her voice, and we all looked out the window to see my father on the deck. He was home early. He'd loosened his tie and fixed himself a drink, and now he settled himself into a lawn chair, shook out the newspaper, and crossed his legs.

'Isn't your father the most predictable person on earth?' my mother said happily. 'Watch this,' and she ate a cherry, spat the pit into her hand, and took aim at my father. It landed on the deck not far from his feet. She did it again, this time hitting the front page. My father glanced up.

'Hey,' he said. 'Cut that out.'

My mother threw a whole cherry at him. He caught it and ate it.

'Okay,' he said. 'That's enough.'

My mother threw another cherry at him.

'You'll stain my shirt,' my father warned.

'Oh Hugh, you big stiff.' My father raised his eyebrows then, stood up, and planted himself in a batting stance with the newspaper rolled up.

When my mother threw another cherry, he swung hard and missed.

'Weak pitch, Mimi,' he said. 'You can do better.'

They played this game while Ellie and I sat and watched, transfixed by this rare show of goofiness. Then my mother stopped shooting cherries and my father let his newspaper drop to the ground and they stared at each other, and he put his hands on his hips, and without breaking his gaze my mother said, 'Will you excuse us for a moment, girls?'

I didn't need Ellie to explain it to me. In fact, if my mother had wanted to flaunt it, like she usually did, I wouldn't have minded. I wouldn't have minded at all.

16

At forty, my mother stood five-six and weighed ninety-eight pounds. She had a bald spot above her left ear from scratching, a pale oval she couldn't disguise any longer with some artful combing and a few bobby pins. She'd stopped buying clothes for herself long ago, and lived in a pair of blue jeans and one of my father's old white shirts, whose tails hung to her knees. People mistook her for our older sister, which pleased her.

All daughters say wicked things to their mothers, things they will later regret, and I was no exception. By twelve, I'd begun to follow Ellie's example by staying away from the house as much as possible. This choice was facilitated by the fact that rumors were circulating among parents in the neighborhood, and already two of my friends had been forbidden to play at my house. My mother let us smoke. My mother let us drink. My mother showed us all of her various contraceptive devices and taught us how to douche and left dirty books lying around. That sort of thing.

I was angry most of the time. Being in a heightened pubescent state, with puffy, tender nipples and a few thin scribbles of hair between my legs, and living in constant fear of a blot on the back of my skirt, I blamed my mother at the get-go for anything and everything. She was an easy target. She didn't fight back, and I would leave our arguments feeling victorious and righteous, if uneasy. Later I would hate her even more, for being so passive. Why couldn't she ever snap back?

As much as I could, I tagged after Ellie, which brought her ridicule from her friends, which she transferred to me. But at home it was different. We would stay up long past our bedtime, painting our toenails Yardley pink and rolling our hair on black wire curlers for the Marlo Thomas flip. We would speculate — rather matter-of-factly — on our mother's mental state. Ellie's theory was that our mother knew she ought to check into a hospital, but didn't want to embarrass us. But Jesus, Ellie said, did she really not know that everyone called her a nutcase?

'Don't let Dad hear that word,' I said.

'Daffy. Loony. What's in a word?'

'Did you see her head was bleeding tonight? Where she scratches?'

'Gross,' said Ellie.

'And she won't put anything on it,' I said. 'Not even a little Bactine. She's scared it will make the rest of her hair fall out.'

'Dad will take care of it,' Ellie said. 'It's not our problem.'

But it was our problem. 'If it gets infected, it's right near the brain,' I said, tears welling in my eyes. 'She could die.'

'She's not going to die, Izzy,' Ellie said. 'Not that way, anyway.'

I wiped my eyes and eased my head back upon my pillow. The curlers felt like golf balls. I never got a lot of sleep when I set my hair. Worse, my mother wouldn't even notice my hair the next morning. Nor would she notice the dress I'd borrowed from a friend, or the nylons I'd begun to wear instead of knee socks, or the fact that I'd started shaving my legs.

It was my shaving, I am convinced, that started the short chain of events that ended up with a forty-one-year-old woman slumped in the front seat of her car. I'd been shaving my legs in the bathtub one day, and had just cut my shin, and was fascinated by the tiny red pinheads forming along my shinbone, the crimson dots that swelled together and dribbled down my leg. It didn't hurt, but the blood was impressive, and right then my mother knocked on the bathroom door.

'I need a Kotex!' she called.

Quickly I dunked my leg. The blood swirled in pink tendrils, which I swished away as my mother opened the door. She hadn't seen me naked in a while, I guess, because she gazed at my body too long, and I detected a fleeting wince, as though she was alarmed by my development. I hated her for that.

She went about her business with the Kotex, dropping her pants to reveal an ugly white bundle between her legs, held up by a dingy elastic belt with metal garters. Her belly was pale, her pubic hair black and spidery. She sat on the toilet, spread her legs, and unhooked the blood-soaked pad, which she mummified in toilet paper. Then she took a clean pad, twisted around to hook it up in back, pulled the front tail through her legs, and hooked it up in front. Standing, she gave the entire contraption an extra tug and a wiggle to settle it into place, and pulled up her pants.

'I see you've got breast buds,' she remarked, leaning toward the mirror to examine something on her nose. 'Pretty soon you'll have to start checking for lumps every month. You can get breast cancer as a teenager, you know. Though it's not very common.'

'I'm fine,' I said darkly. I had no shortage of anger those days, especially after seeing her wince at the sight of my body, and I hated seeing her pubic hair. I went on to suggest that she change her Kotex in private from now on. Normal women had a sense of modesty, I pointed out.

'Oh,' she said. 'And I'm not normal?'

I shrugged, and inspected my wound. The bleeding had stopped.

'I suppose I'm not, am I?' she sighed. 'And I suppose it's hard on you. But you know, Izzy, better to have a mother like me than June Cleaver.'

'I doubt that.'

'That's because you're a teenager,' my mother said. 'When you grow up you'll see it's good to break the mold, even if people think you're a little odd.'

'Odd? Try loony. Try batty.'

'Those are not kind words,' my mother said. 'I can use them, but you can't. Not about me, anyway. I'm your mother.'

I laughed loudly and meanly. 'Right,' and I

bent forward to dig dirt out of my big toenail. 'You know, Mom, you never should have had children,' I remarked.

'Excuse me?'

'You heard.'

'Why?'

'Because you're a ridiculous mother,' I said, looking up. 'You make Ellie and me take care of you, and you grab all the attention, making everyone worry about you. Plus you lie all the time. I wish Dad had married someone else. Then I'd have a real mother. Someone who could think of me once in a while, instead of herself.'

It was about the cruelest thing I could have said, and I was very pleased with myself. Out of the corner of my eye I saw her fingering the hollow of her neck.

'Is that what you really think?'

I shrugged. Maybe I'd gone too far, but I was feeling too good to take back my words. Besides, they held a lot of truth for me.

'Well,' my mother said quietly. 'Aren't we the little bitch today.' She left me then, leaving the bathroom door wide open. I hollered after her to close the door, but she didn't, and I had to climb out and close it myself to regain my privacy.

But I had won. I had gotten my mother to call me a bitch, and she would never forgive herself for that.

As afternoon turned to evening, I began to feel guilty. There was nothing good about saying mean things to people, especially your mother; there was nothing good about taunting them to

165

say mean things back to you. But still I couldn't bring myself to apologize. Not until she apologized for all the ways in which she had failed us.

That night it rained. My father was working late, and it was just the three of us, my mother and Ellie and I, and we poked at our Swanson pot pies in wretched silence at the kitchen table. After dinner my mother got ready for bed, but then it started raining again and I heard her bed creak, and the next thing I knew she was standing out in the alley in her white nightgown, which clung to her legs like wet tissue.

Ellie joined me at the window. 'Is she okay?'

'No, actually,' I told her. 'I said some really mean stuff this afternoon.'

'Like what?'

'Like how bad a mother she is.'

'So what? I tell her that all the time.' But Ellie left the room, and in a minute I saw her running across the lawn, hunched under her raincoat. She huddled with our mother for a long time, and at one point she even put her arm around our mother's shoulder; but eventually my sister came back inside alone.

'She says she's fine,' Ellie said, shaking out her coat.

'Do you believe her?'

'No, but what am I going to do? Drag her in?'

I was relieved when, soon after, my father's headlights beamed up the alley. My mother was still standing in front of the garage. He stopped his car, climbed out, and huddled with her in the shimmering triangle cast by his headlights. I don't know what he said, but finally he led her across the yard and into the kitchen. Ellie quickly shut our bedroom door, and we turned out the lights and hopped into bed.

Through the heating register we could hear the clink of ice cubes, the crackling of cellophane; then, footsteps on the stairs, the sudden knock of pipes, the charge of water filling the tub. I closed my eyes, and imagined my father sitting on the edge of the tub, his sleeves rolled up as he poured water over my mother's back. She would tell him what I'd said, and what she'd said, and he would convince her that neither of us had meant it. Although this scenario would let me off the hook in a way I didn't deserve, it was the way it should be. It was his job, not mine, to patch up the black holes in her moods.

Still, there's a portion of the brain, and I'm sure a scientist could name it, that records word for word a few very select things you've said or heard in your life: the first declaration of love, say, or a doctor's diagnosis. All it takes is for one neuron to fire at the right time, and the tape starts running. *Then I'd have a real mother. You never should have had children.*

It used to be that not a day passed without that tape running in my head, playing back my exact words. But over time, the words began to change, as though some technical editor had gone in and tampered with things, and these days, I'll hear myself tell her she was a bad mother, but I'll add that I love her. Or I'll assure her that although I might wish out loud for a

167

different mother, I don't really mean it.

And at this point, if I am lucky, my mother's gentle, wise voice comes in. *I know you didn't mean what you said, Izzy,* she'll say. *And besides, you're just a child. You don't have to hold me up.* And for a while, I am absolved.

17

By the time we get home it's seven-thirty. I figure I could drink about a case of wine right now. Gabe and my father are already home — the Land Cruiser's in the driveway, and poking out of its back is a green kayak.

The men are both in the kitchen, making spaghetti. Kayak pamphlets litter the kitchen table, and the message light is blinking furiously. Gabe stirs the sauce as my father tears lettuce leaves into a large wooden bowl. They could be a couple, the way they work together.

My father squats to examine Rachel's stitches and Gabe leans to kiss me. 'No surprises at the ER, I take it?' he says.

'She's fine,' I tell him.

'Nice necklace.'

'It's from Ellie,' I say, fingering the silver strands. 'Whose kayak is that out there?'

My father stands up. 'It's mine,' he says proudly. Inwardly I smile at this rare display of impulsiveness.

'Good for you, Dad,' I tell him.

'Go look in the living room, though,' he says, turning back to his salad.

Warily I venture into the living room. There on the rug lies a second kayak, this one blue. Its paddle lies neatly by its side. I run my hands through my hair. My father has always subscribed to the notion that gifts should fill a functional need, which has compelled him over the years to give me a lot of Dustbusters and flannel sheets. A kayak makes me nervous.

'Like it?' he asks from the doorway, wiping his hands on a towel.

I step into the cockpit and squat down. 'Dad, this is too much.'

'Well, you can't have it unless you agree to take lessons. I don't want you rolling over and not being able to bring yourself back up. And you'll need a helmet too. Put your feet there,' and he squats and adjusts my knees. 'See, I got a little demonstration, you sit like this. Boy, these things are tippy!' he says happily. 'I got myself soaked!'

'Very cool gift,' Ellie says, looking on. 'Can't say that mine measures up but hey. Wow.'

I climb out and give my father a hug. 'Thank you,' I tell him.

'Can I get in?' asks Rachel.

'Go ahead,' I say, going back into the kitchen. 'Who called?' I ask Gabe.

Gabe is shaking salt into the sauce. 'Don't know, haven't checked,' he says. 'Anchovies or not?'

'Not,' Ellie and I say in unison.

'Either way,' says my father.

I push the button on our answering machine, and everyone listens. All the messages are from Wilson, each more urgent than the last.

'Oh well,' says Ellie cheerfully. 'Poor Wilson.'

'You want to use the phone in our bedroom?'

'I ain't callin' him,' Ellie says. 'Let the guy wonder. Come on, Rachel,' she says. 'Time to get your nightie on.'

Rachel looks up from the kayak. 'Before dinner?'

'You can eat dinner in your nightie. Go on, do it now.'

Rachel climbs out, but hesitates.

'What are you waiting for?' Ellie demands.

'It's dark.'

'So turn a light on. Don't be such a scaredy cat.'

Gabe, who has been trying to convince my waste-abhoring father to cook two boxes of pasta rather than just one, stops stirring the sauce and wipes his hands. 'Come with me, Rachel,' he says. 'I'll take you down.'

As they leave, Ellie rolls her eyes. 'What'd I tell you? She won't go anywhere alone. Wacko genes, I swear.'

I must be tired, because instead of commiserating I say what I think. 'Would it really be so bad to just give her what she wants tonight?'

'Girls,' my father murmurs.

'Oh, Izzy, please don't play child psychologist with me. You wouldn't believe how much I indulge her, you couldn't even count the number of nights she sleeps in my bed. It's a matter of principle. Sometimes you have to be tough.'

'In a strange house?'

Ellie drops into a kitchen chair and closes her eyes. 'Tell you what, Izzy, when you've got children and they've got problems, then you can give me advice. Okay?'

I swear, upon hearing this tone of voice I feel a cold sore starting, hot and viral and sour as metal.

'Well now, wasn't that a pleasant thing to say to one's sister on her birthday,' Ellie remarks. 'Aren't I a dream tonight. Oh, Christ. All this shit with Wilson's got me talking toads, you know? Hey, I'm sorry. I'll start over. How did he figure out I was here, anyway?'

'Wild guess?'

'Maybe he wants to come back,' Ellie continues. 'No chance of that, though. Huh. No way am I letting that guy back into my life.'

My father turns from the stove. 'Say what?'

Before Ellie has a chance to explain, Rachel appears in the kitchen doorway, dressed for the night in white cotton pajamas printed with colored soccer balls. She wears a somber look and seems hesitant until Ellie opens her arms, and then she climbs safely into her lap. Ellie murmurs something into her ear and Rachel smiles.

'How's your head?' Ellie asks, businesslike.

'Good,' says Rachel. She picks up a fat yellow candle. 'Can I light this?'

'Sure,' and Ellie hands her a pack of matches.

'Uncle Gabe says they have mountain lions here,' says Rachel.

'Uncle Gabe likes to joke,' Ellie says. 'There are no mountain lions here.'

There are, but I don't correct her.

'But if there were, they couldn't get through the windows, could they?' asks Rachel.

'Of course not,' Ellie says.

'Will you lock them anyway?'

'Of course I will.'

'It's not that I'm scared,' Rachel explains to

nobody, bending like Gumby to bite off a piece of toenail. 'I just don't want them coming in my room.'

Ellie nods, and is about to add something when the phone rings. Gabe answers it, and hands it to Ellie, who rolls her eyes but takes the phone.

'Just what I need,' she says. 'Hello, Wilson.'

'It's *Dad*? Calling from *France*? Can I talk?' Rachel tugs at her mother's sleeve. 'Let me talk first!'

Ellie shakes her off, stands up, and goes into the living room. The timer on the stove beeps. My father lifts the pot with two red mitts; steam rises as he drains the pasta into a colander in the sink. 'Problems?' he asks.

'They're splitting up,' I tell him.

He shakes the colander without replying. I swear, sometimes I think he should have been a minister, he can take in the worst news like it's a weather report. 'I knew it,' he finally says, shaking his head. 'They spend too much time apart. He travels too much. He's always off somewhere.'

'So bring out the big guns,' we hear Ellie say from the next room. 'I've got a few myself. Rachel,' she calls, 'your father wants to talk to you.' Coming through the kitchen door, she hands Rachel the phone as though it is contaminated. 'Don't tell him about the roller coaster,' she whispers as Rachel walks off.

'How's Wilson?' my father asks.

Ellie takes out a cigarette. 'He's fine, Pops.' She leans forward to light the cigarette from the

173

candle, then sits back and blows smoke toward the ceiling, her neck long and lumpy in the candlelight.

'You said you quit,' my father says.

'Well, guess what, Dad. I lied.'

I can see a little pulse going in my father's temple. 'Maybe you shouldn't be smoking in your sister's house,' he says.

'Where am I going to go, Pops,' Ellie says calmly. 'I can't smoke inside, I can't smoke outside. You want me to go back to New York? We're splitting up,' she tells him.

'Mom didn't know where I was!' we hear Rachel exclaim. 'She thought I was lost!'

'Hang up now, Rachel,' Ellie calls to her. 'Don't look at me that way, Dad. You knew it was coming.'

Rachel comes back into the kitchen. 'Now he wants to talk to you!' she exclaims, handing me the phone. I glance at Ellie, who merely shrugs.

'So talk to him,' she says. 'I don't give a shit.'

'Don't take too long,' my father says. 'Dinner's ready.'

Outside on the deck, the sweet smell of pine lingers in the air. The night sky is spattered with stars, full of celestial frost. I clear my throat.

'Wilson,' I begin.

Wilson does not waste time. 'How much did she tell you, Izzy?'

'Well, she told me about the one-way ticket.'

'Did she tell you I'm filing for custody?'

I pause. 'Joint, right?'

'Nope.'

A chill travels through my arms. 'Wilson,' and

I have to clear my throat again, 'Wilson, please don't do this.'

'She's not an easy person to live with, you know,' he says. 'And I'm not talking about just me here. I'm talking about Rachel. The things this kid sees, Izzy! Well, you probably know.'

'Wilson,' I say, picturing my sister holding Rachel's head while she got stitches, 'she'd be devastated. She's totally devoted to that child.'

'Not when she's standing on a window ledge she isn't,' Wilson says. 'Not when she's zonked out on Xanax.'

'What window ledge?'

'Oh, she didn't tell you about that? Figures. Though I'm surprised Rachel didn't tell you either.'

'What about the window ledge?'

'Oh, Ellie's just lying on the bed reading to Rachel and suddenly she gets up and swipes all the Beanie Babies off the windowsill and yanks up the window. Out she climbs. This was bedtime, Izzy. A kid's bedtime! I'd told her at dinner I thought a separation would be good and she agreed and I'm thinking, God this is easy, and the next thing I know she's out on the fucking window ledge. With Rachel watching. She can't raise this child, Izzy.'

And I think of a time long ago when I came home from school to find a bowl of M&Ms on the table, along with a note from my mother, telling my father that the girls (Me! I wanted to shout, you left this for me to read, so say my name, say Izzy!) that the girls would be better off if he raised us alone. I remember how my chest

175

tightened at the thought of no mother at home, no rides in the Plymouth, no midnight baths, no dancing in the rain. At that moment I didn't care if my father might do a better job alone. No matter how crazy, she was my mother and I wanted to grow up with her. Was that asking too much? From her? From anyone?

'When did this happen?' I ask Wilson.

'Two weeks ago.'

'And was she on her medication?'

'Oh yes.'

'She'll fight you,' I tell him. 'You know that, don't you? And you're going to have to prove she's unfit. How are you going to do that? Who are you going to get to testify?'

The phone hums.

'Oh no,' I say. 'No, no, no. Forget it, Wilson. Don't do this to me.'

'Think about Rachel,' he says calmly. 'Don't think about yourself.'

'Rachel would be blown away!'

'Maybe for a while. But then she'd get on with a normal life. Which she doesn't have now, that's for sure — unless you think it's normal for a seven-year-old to talk her mother out of jumping off a window ledge. Maybe that's normal in your family, but not mine.'

His words chisel a hole in my heart. It's as if he has skimmed through my mental diary, and read what I wished for so many times as a child. I didn't want my mother gone, one hundred percent — but maybe if my parents had gotten divorced? What if our father had raised us, weekdays with him, every other weekend with her, our visits always closely supervised? Maybe I wouldn't have grown up hating her as much as loving her. Maybe I wouldn't have felt pushed to say the awful things I said.

And maybe none of what happened would have happened.

'I know it puts you on the spot,' he says. 'I know it's not fair but you have to think about Rachel here, not Ellie.'

'Does Ellie know you're asking me to do this?'

'Not yet.'

'Well please don't say anything tonight. It's not the best time, you know.'

'Sorry.'

'I mean, it's my birthday.'

'Sorry. Happy birthday. Don't you say anything, either. I'd just as soon keep this under wraps until she gets back.' There is a pause. 'It's not like I'd take her off to Siberia, you know,' he adds. 'I'd stay in New York.'

'That doesn't help a whole lot.'

'Think about it,' he says.

After hanging up, I lean against the railing for a moment. High in the sky, a nighthawk makes its bulleted plunge, you can't see it but you can hear it, a sharp honk as it swoops within feet of the trees. I imagine myself on a witness stand, being cross-examined about Ellie's mothering skills. Isn't it true that she lets the child eat marshmallows in bed? That she talks about sex in front of her? That she calls her a scaredy cat?

Maybe so, but —

And isn't it true that she threatened to jump

off a window ledge, right in front of the girl?

Oh for Christ's sake, I hear Ellie say to me. I wasn't serious about jumping and the only reason I did it was to make Wilson feel bad for leaving me. I told her that. She wasn't scared. She knows me.

'Isabel?'

I turn to see my father's silhouette in the doorway. His back problems have worsened over the years, and he compensates by tilting his shoulders, like a poorly crafted scarecrow.

'Are you off the phone?' he asks.

I want to ask him if he ever threatened to take us away from our mother. And if she ever threatened things in return. She would have had Nana's money and Nana's help, whereas my father, with no extended family and a full-time job and a mortgage and three dependents and stacks of case law against him, would have had a difficult task ahead of him.

'Come on in,' he says, 'we're all hungry and frankly I'm kind of concerned about this little mess we've got on our hands.'

He gestures with a cock of his head; but I do not see him, because suddenly I am a thousand miles away, riding a train through the night. Another train is approaching on a parallel track, its headlight a tiny star that grows larger and brighter, the locomotive suddenly taking form, the thundering roar as darkened cars flash by. Then, in slow motion, a lighted car floats past. I look closely and see my mother's face in the window. Ellie and I are asleep next to her, our small bodies folded against each other. Seeing

178

the other me, my mother lowers her eyes, stubs out her cigarette, and draws her children close. She smoothes stray bangs off our foreheads. It is a long night ahead of her, a long journey, and she will let no one disturb their fragile slumber.

All good mothers love, and try their best.

'Sweetheart,' my father says, 'you worry me, out here alone like this,' which is the last thing I want to do. I let the train speed up, let it pass me in the night, and go inside to where my family waits.

18

A couple of nights after the shaving incident, my family went out to dinner at the Space Needle to celebrate a case my father had won. My mother got very drunk, an easy thing for her to do, given her weight and the fact that she never ate anything at restaurants. One martini and she was looped. Halfway into the dinner she said she was going to the ladies' room, but she didn't come back for a long time and my father and Ellie and I suddenly stopped talking and just looked at one another, all three at once, and we pushed back our chairs and hurried out to the observation deck expecting to find her on the other side of the railing, ready to jump. But after two laps we still couldn't find her, and we returned — still anxious — to the dining room, only to find her sitting calmly at our table, smoking and flirting with the waiter. She wore a white sleeveless shift two sizes too big; her arms looked like chicken wings sticking out of the armholes. While my father scolded her, she twirled a strand of hair and winked at Ellie and me. Nothing was real about her, it seemed. Where we were, she wasn't.

A week later, she realized it was almost her birthday. 'Forty-one, girls!' she exclaimed, glancing at the calendar. 'Yikes! That used to seem so old,' she sighed. 'When Nana was forty-one she had saggy bosoms. Do I look forty-one? I don't think I look forty-one at all.'

Then in the next breath, she began criticizing women who couldn't admit their age. 'You see these gals in their miniskirts, dying their hair, trying to look like they're still in their twenties,' she scoffed. 'Not me. The older I get the better I get — hell, when I was twenty I couldn't manage three orgasms in a row.'

My father asked what she wanted to do for her birthday. Being in one of her up moods, she said she didn't care about the specifics but wanted something very very special, because frankly she hadn't expected to make it to age forty-one, and no, she wasn't trying to make us uncomfortable but we might as well not try to hide the past, did a certain rainy evening and a certain bottle of pills ring a bell, and here she was, well on her way to half a decade. She wanted to celebrate.

While she was taking her bath that night, my father summoned Ellie and me into the kitchen to plan my mother's forty-first birthday party. He would buy lobsters, he said. And champagne. Maybe some raw oysters beforehand? Oh, and a cake, of course — Ellie could order something from the bakery. Me, I was to decorate the table. Use the silver, my father said. And Nana's tablecloth.

Nana wasn't doing very well these days. She'd had a series of small strokes over the past year, which kept her from traveling. I missed her, number one because of all the gifts she brought and the food she cooked, and number two because her presence made my mother act normal. I wanted to call her and say, here's a plane ticket, come out for a birthday party

181

— just so my mother would put on some decent clothes and lipstick. So she would raise the shades in her bedroom and vacuum out the car. We'd bought a Dodge Dart after my mother sank the Plymouth, pale blue with a push-button transmission, but my mother scorned the car and trashed it with candy wrappers and soda cans.

'Too bad Nana couldn't be here,' I said.

'We could send her a plane ticket,' Ellie suggested.

'Nana doesn't fly,' our father reminded us. 'Besides, Nana needs a full-time nurse these days.'

'We can make things normal, though,' I murmured.

My father glanced at me over the top of his glasses. 'We can make things normal,' he said. 'We don't need Nana to be a family.'

I was glum and worried. I had mixed feelings about taking part in any celebration on my mother's behalf. I knew that her birthday would force me to make some kind of amends, but there were still toads on the tip of my tongue, and no apology forthcoming. That night I lay awake in bed and tried composing a note in my head. *Dear Mother*, it read. *The other day I said some things. I'm sorry.* Then my mind went blank. Was that really all I could say? How sullen it sounded. How flat.

I slept on it, and the next day during study period, I drafted a more substantial letter in my notebook. *Dear Mom*, I wrote. *I know you haven't forgotten the things I said the other day, in the bathroom. I'm sorry for hurting you. That was wrong. I hope you can be well, because there is really no one else I want for a mother.*

Rereading my words, my throat began to ache and swell, and I had to excuse myself to go to the girls' room before anyone could see me cry. Friends knew something was wrong with my mother, but they didn't know the details, and I didn't want questions. It would only mean more lies.

That afternoon I stopped at the drugstore, and found a card with purple lilacs (her favorite flower) on the front and a blank parchment lining inside. No stupid poems, no corny messages. At home I sequestered myself in my room and transcribed the note directly onto the parchment, using my father's Cross pen and my best handwriting, and taking great care to make no mistakes. When I was finished, I slipped the card into its envelope, sealed it with a drop of wax, and hid it beneath my underwear in my top bureau drawer. Already I felt half forgiven.

On the morning of her birthday, my mother, who usually slept late and let my father get us off to school, came shuffling into the kitchen while we were all eating oatmeal. Frumpy in my father's plaid flannel bathrobe, she poured a cup of coffee, lit a cigarette, sat down at the table as though she got up like this every morning of her life and looked at Ellie and me and said in a husky voice, 'Good morning, precious ones.'

'Happy birthday,' Ellie said.

'Happy birthday, Mom,' I echoed.

'Forty-one!' my father exclaimed with a forced lilt in his voice. 'Happy birthday, Mimi!'

My mother dragged hungrily on her cigarette and peered into my bowl. 'Oatmeal, Hugh,' she remarked. 'How special.'

'I wasn't expecting you for breakfast.'

'Not even a few donuts?'

'There's pancake mix,' he offered.

'I hate pancakes, Hugh,' my mother said. 'Seventeen years and you still don't know what I like and don't like. Guess I'll just have to have the usual toast,' she sighed, rising from the table.

Without answering, my father stood up and ran water into the pasty oatmeal pot. I felt sorry for him, and wished my mother had stayed in bed. Why such a bad mood? Why this morning? Couldn't she match mood to occasion, just once?

My father cleared his throat and told us he had a meeting at nine, so he'd better get going.

'You can't be a little teeny tiny bit late?' my mother said, buttering her toast. 'Even a half-hour?'

'Honey,' he said, 'we're due in court at ten and we have to go over the testimony first.'

My mother turned away and dropped her knife into the sink. She began to sing a song that was popular on the radio around that time, about a well-respected man about town. 'Well he gets up in the morning,' she sang. 'And he goes to work each day.'

'Tonight,' my father promised, as he kissed her on the cheek. 'All right? We'll make some time tonight?'

'Maybe,' she said, inspecting her nails, 'although the mood may have passed.'

184

'What will you do today?' he asked.

'Oh, I don't know. Get my hair done. Fix the drain. Caulk up the cracks in the garage.'

I cleared my bowl and fingered through the change jar for lunch money.

'What's that for?' my mother demanded.

'Lunch,' I told her.

'It's not cigarette money, is it?'

'I told you,' I said. 'It's for lunch.'

'Good,' she said. 'Don't ever smoke. It's a nasty habit. Goddamn coffin nails,' she said, stubbing out her cigarette in my father's bowl.

'See you after school,' I said on my way out the door.

'If I'm here.'

'Well, see you whenever, then.'

It was mid-March, and the rhododendrons were bursting into bloom, gaudy snowballs of purple and pink that drooped with last night's rain. This was Nana's favorite time of year, and I found myself wishing again that she could be here, if only to shut my mother up.

'Why does he stay with her?' I said to Ellie as we walked to school.

'I don't know. I'd be out the door the next day,' Ellie declared. 'I don't know how he puts up with her.'

'Good sex, I guess.'

'So we're told.'

'Too often,' I added. 'I hate it when she talks about sex.'

'Well, brace yourself, kiddo,' Ellie said.

At school I lost myself in tests, reports, and gym, where we had to play crab soccer, an awful game where you skittered around with your pelvis hoisted off the floor, trying to kick a huge gray ball. I didn't think about my mother until after school, when Ellie told me she was going to a friend's house and she would pick up the cake on her way home.

I had a lot of homework, so when I walked up the alley and saw my mother's car gone, I thought: Good. I can get a lot done. Inside, I set my books on the table, made myself a honey sandwich, and went upstairs.

I loved being in the house when it was empty. I opened our window to wash away the stale air, and along with the fresh breeze came the sound of hammering in the distance, birds singing, the smell of mud — a day of beginnings, with nobody around but myself. I did my homework subject by subject: a few pages of history, a book report for English, a set of math problems. Check, check, done.

My father called at five to see if my mother was home. No, I told him. Good, he said, he was going to leave work now and pick up the lobsters. Had I set the table yet? Had Ellie gotten the cake? I promised him that everything would be ready by the time he got home.

I cleared a week's worth of newspapers from the dining room table and spread out Nana's blue embroidered tablecloth. I set out plates, and silverware, and napkins. I got out the silver lobster picks and the porcelain butter dishes from Germany. I put new white candles in the heavy brass candlesticks. Finally I went upstairs and got the card I'd written, and came back down and set it on my mother's plate.

I hope she doesn't read it out loud, I thought.

At five-thirty Ellie came home with the box from the bakery, which, when opened, revealed a large round chocolate cake, with the words 'Happy Birthday, Mother' scripted in pink. Very carefully Ellie removed it from the box and set it on Nana's silver cake plate, which she put in the center of the table. When she wasn't looking I swiped my finger through one of the glossy peaks and stuck it into my mouth. How sweet, how creamy!

At six o'clock my father arrived home. He laid his briefcase by the kitchen table, as he always did, and hung his coat in the front hall closet, loosened his tie, came back to the kitchen, washed his hands, and drank a glass of water. He told Ellie to go get the lobsters, which he'd left in the back seat of his car.

'Where's your mother?' he asked me.

'I don't know,' I said. 'Did you see the table?'

'It looks beautiful, honey.'

'Mom was in a bad mood this morning, wasn't she?' I ventured.

'She's always in a bad mood when she gets up early,' he said. 'I took her out to lunch, though, and we were able to have a little time together.' Hearing this, I smiled to myself. According to Ellie, 'a little time together' in my father's words meant sex. Unlike my mother, he didn't like to flaunt things.

'Look at those guys!' he exclaimed, peering into the box Ellie had set down on the table. 'Lively little fellas, aren't they? Let's get a pot of water boiling,' he said happily. 'Ellie, chop me some celery. Izzy, you get the butter out and start making garlic bread. Gosh — I hate to say this but isn't it nice we don't have to worry about Wally? Remember how Wally used to snitch food as soon as we turned our backs?'

'I kind of miss Wally, actually,' I said.

'I don't,' Ellie declared. 'Wally was a royal pain.'

'I don't miss Wally stealing ten bucks' worth of meat every week,' my father admitted. 'I don't miss Wally chewing up my shoes.'

I flashed on Wally chasing seagulls, loping through tall beach grass and collapsing every night at the foot of his owner's bed. 'Maybe we could get another dog,' I said.

'I'm not cleaning up dog shit,' Ellie said.

'All you remember is the bad stuff,' I told her.

'I'm a realist.'

'Don't we like to use big words,' I said. 'Aren't we in the famous ninth grade.'

'Girls,' my father said.

'Are these oysters?' asked Ellie, peering into a paper bag.

'They sure are,' my father said, 'and you can start shucking them while I make French fries.'

With an enormous clatter, Ellie dumped the oysters into the sink and turned on the water. She and my mother, the only ones who liked raw oysters, were the only ones who knew how to fix them — a dangerous procedure, I thought, watching Ellie grasp the rocky shell in one hand and work at prying it open with a stubby knife.

All that effort just to swallow a mouthful of slime.

As Ellie shucked oysters, my father opened up the sack of potatoes and began peeling them onto a sheet of newspaper, his hips jiggling as he whisked away. Maybe this is what it's all about, I thought. You meet someone, you fall in love, you marry them. You buy a house, you peel potatoes for their birthday, you pick them up after they swallow a bunch of pills.

My father glanced at his watch and frowned. 'Did your mother leave a note?'

'No,' I said.

'She should be back by now,' he said as he started to peel another potato. 'I wonder if she went shopping or something.' But his speculation was cut off by a sudden shriek as the oyster knife flew up in the air and Ellie careened back from the counter clutching her hand.

'Fuck oh fuck oh fuck!' she screamed, and my father dropped the potato and reached out to grab her, but he tripped on the sack of potatoes that he'd left on the floor and they both lurched against the stove.

'I don't want a booster shot!' Ellie screamed.

'Calm down, let me — '

'Not a booster shot, please not a booster shot!'

'I said calm down!' he roared, and he yanked her hand out to reveal a meaty hole in her palm, with what looked like rubber bands sticking out. Blood dripped onto the floor.

'Oh Daddy please no booster shot please!' she screamed, and frankly I thought she was being a bit of a baby and was about to say as much when

189

my father told me to run and get the first aid kit. I dashed up the stairs and in the bathroom found a shoebox labeled 'First Aid,' but all it contained were a few Band-Aids and a tube of K-Y jelly.

'That's it?' my father exclaimed when I showed him. 'That's all you could find? What does your mother clean your cuts with?'

'Bleach,' I told him.

'Clorox?'

'It kills germs,' I said.

'Oh God,' he said. 'Don't let her put bleach on your cuts, honey, okay? It's not a very good thing to do. Go get some ice, would you? We'll ice this thing,' he told Ellie, who was beginning to shake. 'Calm down. We'll ice it and get you up to the emergency room.'

'I don't want a shot,' Ellie whimpered.

'Will she get a shot?' I asked him.

'I don't know,' my father said. 'Just go get the ice — I bought a whole bag last night for the oysters, it's out in the other refrigerator. Hold your hand up,' he told Ellie. 'That's a girl.'

Outside in our backyard, the air was damp and rooty-smelling, the ground spongy from all the rain. Slugs glistened like small fish in the grass. At the alley's edge our camellia was still in bloom, its white rosettes reflecting the pale light from the kitchen window.

I glanced down the alley hoping to see my mother's car driving up, but all was dark. Typical of her to keep us waiting like this, I thought as I bent to grasp the handle at the base of the garage's overhead door. Make us wait, make us worry, then breeze in like nothing happened.

190

I tugged at the handle, but the door was cemented to the ground. I pulled again, pulled as hard as I could until my stomach burned. It's locked, stupid, I thought, straightening up. Try the side door. I made my way around the garage to the side door, but it too wouldn't budge.

We never locked the garage doors.

In the kitchen, my father was sitting in a chair with Ellie balanced on his knees, her long legs stretched out as she rested back against his chest. When I came in, she frowned and raised her injured hand up over her head. Ellie was such a milker.

'I need the key,' I told my father.

'Why?'

'The doors are locked.'

'They're never locked.'

'They are tonight.'

'Give the side door a shove,' he said. 'It's probably just stuck.'

I went back out, and this time I gave the side door a shove with my shoulder, twice. Nothing happened. I went back inside and told my father we should just forget about the ice and take Ellie to the hospital. A shadow crept across his face then, nothing you could actually see with your eyes but you could feel it, you could taste it, like the air before a storm.

He stood up, and taking his keys off the little rack by the door, he went outside and strode across the grass. By the side door he held his keys up to the light, then stuck one into the lock, turned, and pushed. He jiggled the handle and pushed again. He gave the door a kick, and

191

shoved with his shoulder, and the rotting doorjamb finally cracked and gave way.

There was the Dodge Dart, its engine gently putting. And there was my mother, slumped against the driver's window.

I heard a whimpering sound I assumed came from my mother. She'll be too sick to eat lobster tonight, I thought, and they'll spoil, and we'll have wasted all that money. My father yanked open the driver's door and dragged my mother out through the side door like some kind of carcass. He knelt down with her, he slapped her face, pressed his fingers to her neck, slapped her again and again and again. The whimpering — which I realized came from my father, not my mother — had grown into a kind of moaning now, like that of a wounded animal, and he grabbed her shoulders and shook and when he pulled her up against his chest, her head fell back like that of an old doll. He cradled her head and stared into her face and gave her one long last ferocious shake, and then the sound from his throat broke free into a roar of grief, filling the rafters, escaping through the roof to the madrona trees outside and the hills of Seattle and the black night sky above.

★   ★   ★

The rest of the night blurs together. Ellie never did get stitched up, because when she eventually saw the doctor the next day, he told her that the gouge was too ragged for stitches. It would have to heal on its own. Which it did, and she was left with a scar, a pale dendrite right in the middle of her palm.

'Makes me feel like Jesus,' she'll say.

Nobody slept at all that night, but I passed the time in Ellie's bed, both of us careful not to touch but positively petrified to lie more than a few inches away from each other. She lay with her bandaged hand across the top of the pillow, and I remember taking great care not to move my head, to avoid bumping her. Through the window I kept looking for the shadow of Mount Rainier but it was pitch black. I closed my eyes and prayed for the mountain to appear, prayed for it to be solstice, for it to be any time but now. There were voices downstairs in the kitchen, police probably, because every so often their murmurs were punctuated by a raspy radio; I could smell coffee, and sometime around dawn the phone started ringing, and thus began the second half of our lives.

19

'So, what,' says Ellie, 'you're saying I'm a bad mother?' It's past midnight, and everyone else is in bed. The fans are still. A soft breeze carries the scent of lavender up from the rock garden. It would have been a peaceful moment, except for the fact that I just told my sister that Wilson was seeking sole custody and wanted me to testify for him. That I didn't laugh hysterically at this prospect has her convinced that I am in fact going to take his side, even though that is not the case.

'I'm not saying you're a bad mother,' I reply. 'But could you tell me about the window ledge?'

Ellie smiles to herself. 'That Wilson,' she says, shaking her head. 'God, he can lie better than both of us put together, can't he?' Then, instead of elaborating, she begins emptying her purse onto the table: mascara and lipstick, a little French dictionary, a pocketknife, a small blue spiral notebook, Lysol wipes, a twisted bag of M&Ms, a silver cigarette lighter, and two passports. When the purse is empty, she upends it and shakes crumbs onto my floor.

'So it's not true?'

'Isabella,' my sister sighs, 'you can't believe everything people tell you.'

'Why would he make this up?'

'Anything to get custody, I guess,' she says. 'I

194

bet he didn't tell you about the Internet stuff, though.'

'What Internet stuff?'

'You definitely don't want to know,' Ellie declares. 'Think 'little girls' and you can put it together.' She unzips her wallet and starts pulling out receipts and photos. 'Hey, look at this,' and she shows me a photo of Rachel in a purple leotard, doing a full split on a balance beam. 'One of her more graceful moments. Hey — remember those dance lessons we took? What was her name?'

'Nance,' I say. 'Rhymes with dance.'

'Wasn't she a Nazi,' Ellie says, slipping the pictures back into the wallet.

'What do you mean, 'little girls'?'

Ellie raises her eyebrows like a know-it-all. 'Let's just say it's a blessing the only reason the Feds paid him a visit was for tax code violations,' she says. 'Wilson has a lot to be grateful for, that's what I think. Of course, if he files for custody, a lot of this might have to come out, wouldn't it?'

I don't envy Wilson, having my sister as an opponent. 'So did you?'

'Did I what?'

'Climb out on a window ledge.'

Ellie tips her head back and laughs. 'You really think — '

'Ellie,' I say, 'did you?'

When she finally meets my gaze, her eyes have gone flat and beady. She crosses her arms and looks away. 'I was pissed.'

'So you threatened to jump off a window

ledge? Are you nuts?'

'Nobody took it seriously.'

'We took it seriously,' I say with burning fury. 'When Mom swallowed all those pills we took it very seriously, if you recall.'

'Well, we were right to take it seriously. Look, she went and actually did it. I won't.'

'How's Rachel supposed to know that?'

'Because she knows I love her.'

'And Mom didn't love us?'

Ellie draws up her knees and grasps her ankles. She is so small she could fit into a laundry basket. 'If she loved us, she never would have left us.'

I swear, the mentally ill could write their ticket to the Supreme Court, with their inborn argumentative skills, their sneaky logic.

'She loved us,' I say thickly.

'Oh yeah? Then why'd she kill herself?'

'She was miserable. You can love your children and still be miserable, can't you? Plus it doesn't help when they make it worse for you.'

'You're saying it was our fault?'

'We weren't exactly the nicest kids, near the end,' I point out. 'And I didn't have to say the things I said.'

'Oh Bella,' Ellie says wearily. 'It wasn't what you said that made her do it. That is so silly. Is that what you've thought, all these years?'

A lump swells in my throat. We've not talked of this in twenty-eight years, not since the night of the last rain dance, when we stood looking out of our bedroom window at our mother, standing in the mist like a child too tired to know when it's time to come in.

'That's a shitload of baggage to carry around,' Ellie remarks.

It occurs to me that both my sister and I are laying some kind of claim — and have been, all these years — to an eventual understanding of what exactly prompts a person to swallow the pills, or seal up the garage, or swim past the breakers. And who are we to know? Just the daughters of a forty-one-year-old woman with secrets in her heart and a virulent mess in her head that nobody in the world will ever understand — not me, not Ellie, not my father or Nana or even quite possibly my mother's own soul.

'Could you at least tell me what happened that night?' I ask.

Reluctantly, and with great drama, Ellie tells me her version, which is much the same as Wilson's, except she claims that she didn't climb out on the ledge but rather just sat in the window with her legs dangling out. It seems like an important distinction for her.

'So there it is,' says Ellie. 'Are you still going to take his side?'

'I never said I was.'

'You're on the fence, though.'

'Bullshit.' How can I be on the fence? Regardless of what my sister has done, she doesn't deserve to have her own child taken away from her. Take Wilson's side? Is she kidding?

I'm on the fence.

The look of disbelief on my sister's face both humiliates and infuriates me. 'Well,' she finally says, 'I guess you do what you have to do. Lucky you,' she says. 'Nice of Wilson, isn't it, to put you on the spot like this.'

★ ★ ★

When I slip between the sheets, Gabe draws his pillow around his head and curls away from me. I yearn to wake him and ask for his advice, but he does not take well to being denied a smooth journey into unconsciousness.

'Gabe,' I whisper into his shoulder blade. 'Gabe, are you awake?'

I know what he would say. He would tell me not to take sides. Stay out of it, he would say. It's your sister's life. You don't have to fix things for her. You're not responsible.

But I am. She is my sister. And he doesn't understand the concept: that as sisters we may keep one hand in our pocket, but always the other hand outstretched, fingertips touching, always.

★ ★ ★

On Sunday morning I wake up to what first sounds like an animal whimpering below our deck. I listen more closely, and realize it is the sound of Rachel crying. I hear my sister's voice, a low muffled alto, and soon the crying stops.

In the kitchen Gabe has made coffee and my father is sitting at the table, the Sunday paper spread out before him. It's mostly ads, but he picks through them, evaluating bargains a

198

thousand miles from home. He's got his orange juice and his vitamin pills lined up, a baggie of oat bran, his glaucoma drops, and an ancient tube of some salve he uses when he feels a cold sore coming on.

'Morning, Isabel,' he says, taking off his glasses. 'Sleep well?'

'I slept fine,' I tell him as I pour myself coffee. 'How about you?'

'Oh, every night I have to get up a couple of times. Then maybe it was one or two but I heard this awful noise! Like a woman screaming!'

'Mountain lions,' Gabe informs him. 'They're mating.'

'Good lord,' my father mutters, disturbed that he has unwittingly brought up the subject of sex.

'So! What's the plan today?' Gabe asks.

Well, for starters I'd like Wilson to call back and tell me that the whole thing with the window ledge never happened. I'd like Ellie to take me aside and tell me that she and Wilson spoke over the phone in the wee hours of the night and agreed a divorce was a big mistake, they really did love one another and things would work themselves out because after all there was a child to think of. I'd like my father and Gabe to get some of the mistletoe pruned. And finally, I'd like to take Rachel to the Children's Museum, where we could connect wires and paint our faces and try to count the hundreds of thousands of us in the triangular mirrored closets.

'I don't care,' I say. 'Maybe — well good morning, sweetheart,' I say as Rachel comes into the kitchen. Her pajamas, tight and fresh the

199

night before, now droop all over from a night of heavy sleeping. The two stitches above her eye look like tiny black bugs.

'Hi,' says Rachel. 'Can we have donuts?'

'What in God's name was that noise last night?' Ellie asks, yawning. She's wearing the old red plaid bathrobe that our mother used to confiscate from our father, only now it's threadbare, and ragged at the hem. 'Sounded like someone getting murdered. Got any Sweet'N Low?'

Her nonchalance makes me wonder if our conversation last night wasn't such a big deal. Maybe she's put it behind her.

Then she says, 'So, d'ja call Wilson yet?' and it's the way she says it — snappy and flippant — that reassures me that yes, our conversation was in fact a big deal and no, we're not finished.

'I don't need to call Wilson,' I say.

'Just checking,' she says. 'Don't be so touchy, Isabel — God, I'm the one who should be touchy, with everyone conspiring against me.'

'Well, I don't need to call him,' I say.

'Fine by me,' and she shrugs. 'Have some Cheerios, Rachel. *Quelle belle journée*,' she exclaims. 'I bet it's fifty degrees cooler this morning, don't you?'

Maybe not fifty, but fall has arrived. Overnight the light has thinned, and the grasses are rich with shades of gold and blue. I glance down the hillside, and there on another one of his wide flat rocks sits our fox. Straight-backed, he watches over the valley, switching his white-tipped tail in a languid, sanguine arc. At a time like this, the

200

simplicity of life in the animal kingdom stands as an enviable model of social behavior.

Sitting around the kitchen table we discuss the day's possibilities: a hike, a picnic, maybe a long lunch at a restaurant. Ellie wants to go hang gliding and when Gabe tells her there is not enough wind, she pouts. When all is said and done, all of these planned activities seem like too much, and we agree it would be better to just hang out at the house, since time is short.

'Fine by me,' Ellie says. 'Come on, Rache, time for your bath.'

'Is Dad going to jail?' Rachel asks as they leave the room.

'No, no, no,' Ellie tells her. Then she says something else that I can't hear.

'What does she mean, everyone conspiring against her?' my father asks.

I don't want to go into it right now, Wilson wanting custody and all. 'I'm not sure,' I tell him.

Troubled, my father gathers up the newspaper. 'You know, it's always something with that gal, isn't it? Well, maybe she'll go into it later. Actually I've got some papers I'd like you to look at,' and he leaves and comes back with a binder. I look at the title.

'Your will?'

'Death and taxes, honey.'

'This isn't my line of work, Dad.'

'Nor mine,' he agrees, 'which is why I had another attorney draw it up for me. But I still want to go over it with you to make sure I'm not missing anything. Do you and Gabe have a will?'

201

'Not yet.'

'You should.'

'Right. And we should refinance the house and consolidate our accounts and pick out some better mutual funds.'

'Just a gentle reminder,' my father says. 'Here, take a look.'

As I leaf through the pages, Ellie comes back upstairs, having left Rachel in the bathtub. Her shorts are rumpled and baggy. If I had to guess, I'd say she lost several pounds during the night.

She blows her nose. 'What's that?'

'Dad's will,' I tell her.

She folds at the waist and grasps her ankles and mumbles something from upside down. I tell her I didn't quite catch what she said.

She straightens up, face red. 'I said, family's getting kind of lopsided, isn't it?'

'What's that supposed to mean?' My father's voice remains patient, as though he is accustomed to missing out on jokes.

'Nothing, Pop,' I tell him.

But he has detected something in Ellie's voice. 'Well for heaven's sake, Ellie, I'm not hiding anything,' he scolds fondly. 'You can see the will too. I'm leaving everything to the two of you. It's no secret. I just thought that since Izzy's a lawyer, she could make sure everything's in order.'

Ellie licks jam off a knife. 'Nah. I trust the two of you,' she says. 'This jam is really good. I must be getting my period because all I want is sweet stuff. I know you hate talking about female shit, Dad, but did you know I've been getting my

202

period every twenty-two days? Three tampons an hour, too! You think it's ovarian cancer?'

'See a doctor,' my father says darkly.

'Right. One of these days.' Ellie sighs. 'I wish Mom had stuck around and gone through menopause so I'd know what was normal.'

The room bleeds with wounded silence. 'That was completely inappropriate,' my father finally says.

'Sorry,' she says, eyes wide, Betty Boopish. 'Sorry sorry sorry!'

My father gathers up his papers. 'You're forty-three,' he says with marked disgust: 'You could learn to keep a few thoughts to yourself in present company.'

This seems to amuse Ellie. 'Yeah, I guess Mom and I were always lacking in that department, weren't we?'

'It's hardly genetic,' my father notes.

'I wouldn't bet my life on that,' says Ellie. 'Hey Dad, did you hear how Wilson's seeking custody?'

'Well, that doesn't surprise me. He's a good father, he's always been involved with Rachel.'

'He certainly has,' says Ellie. She places four chocolate chips on the blade of the jammy knife. 'The thing is, he's seeking sole custody,' and she slips the knife into her mouth, then slides it out clean. 'As in, he's fit and I'm not.'

My father regards her over the top of his glasses. 'He can't do that.'

Ellie won't look at me, which makes me suspect an agenda on her part. 'Sure he can,' she says. 'Of course, I could file for sole custody myself. After all, here I've taken my daughter on a wholesome family trip while he's off fucking some bimbo on the Riviera.'

My father closes his eyes. Count to ten, he always told us. 'What grounds does he have?' he asks. 'Is it your psychiatric health? Is that what he's focusing on?'

'Don't know, Pop,' Ellie says.

'Because heck, everybody's got problems. You seem to be managing pretty well these days, correct me if I'm wrong.' And then, uncannily, he glances in my direction.

'Am I wrong?' he says, looking from me to Ellie and back to me again. 'Is there something else I need to know about?'

'Go ahead,' I tell Ellie.

'What's going on?' my father says.

Ellie scrapes the last of the jam from the jar. 'Oh, Wilson's got this idea that I behave inappropriately in front of Rachel,' and she tells him yet another version of the window-ledge story, this time with her merely opening the window and leaning out a little too far to catch a breath of fresh air.

It's my cue to speak up, to correct things. Secrets are wrong. Secrets are bad. For some reason, I can't speak.

'That won't persuade a judge,' my father says.

'Tell that to Izzy,' Ellie says. 'She's going to testify for Wilson.'

'I never said that!'

'Why would you testify for Wilson?' my father asks me, and when I don't reply he adds, 'How come I get the feeling there's something you two aren't telling me?'

Ellie still won't look at me. Leaning out, stepping out, falling out — it all blurs together, and I wonder if this is the problem Ellie has. Perhaps it's not a conscious lie. Perhaps everyone's exaggerating, even Wilson. I glance at my father and notice this little fold of skin hanging down over his left eye. For some reason it makes me want to cry. It also makes me want to run away from all this. Who am I to distill it all, and tell my aging father just what I think is true and what is not?

'It's complicated,' I say.

My father eyes me critically, taking my words as a sign that I want to discuss it in private, later, which I don't. 'Does Rachel know he's doing this?' he asks.

'Of course not!' Ellie exclaims. 'And don't tell her, either. When a kid thinks her father's God, she doesn't need everyone telling her what an asshole he is.'

'Choice of words, honey?'

'Sorry, Pop.'

He sweeps crumbs into his hand. 'What's this about a girlfriend?'

Ellie ventures, 'I don't think it's love.'

Maybe not, but I can tell that my father is nevertheless bothered by any man's rejection of his daughter.

'And Rachel unfortunately has seen some pretty inappropriate things,' Ellie goes on. 'I don't need to be specific but — '

'Go no further,' my father says darkly.

'Well she knows about it because of Monica Lewinsky, but to see her own father — '

'Ellie!' He continues to glare at her, and I suspect she realizes she has taken things one step too far. In the silence that follows, we hear Rachel calling. With exaggerated politeness, Ellie excuses herself, and when she is gone my father and I clear the plates and load the dishwasher.

'I take it I'm not getting the whole story here,' he says.

'Well,' I say, 'Wilson's version was a little different,' and I tell him Wilson's version of the incident on the window ledge. 'I don't know who to believe,' I say.

'Oh, don't be blind, Isabel.' There's a condescending note in his voice that shames me.

'You think it was as bad as Wilson says?'

'Of course I do.'

'Should we step in?'

Before my father can answer, Gabe walks in and sits down at the kitchen table. He has the checkbook to our savings account, and opens it up. 'Where's Ellie?' he asks, writing.

'Right here,' says Ellie, back now with Rachel, who is wrapped in a worn beach towel. 'What's up?'

Gabe writes out a check and hands it to Ellie.

'What's this?' she says.

'I'm not going to ask about this one,' my father mutters, wiping the counter.

'Part of the money we owe,' Gabe tells Ellie.

'It was a gift, Gabriel,' Ellie says.

'Not in his mind,' I tell her.

'We'll repay it over the next couple of years,' Gabe says.

Ellie shrugs and takes the check. I am terrified she's going to rip it in two, but she doesn't. She tucks it in her back pocket and turns to me. 'Why'd you tell him, anyway?' she asks. 'I thought you were perfectly comfortable keeping it a secret.'

'Well, I changed my mind,' I say. 'I don't like keeping secrets from my husband.'

'I do,' Ellie declares. 'Secrets are good.'

'Maybe that's why you're getting divorced and I'm not.'

'Secrets are fundamentally necessary,' Ellie goes on. 'People shouldn't always feel like they have to disclose everything. I mean, come on. Do I really have to tell Wilson who I think about fucking when we're fucking each other?'

My father makes a gargling sound.

'Sorry,' says Ellie. 'Sorry sorry sorry sorry — '

'Shut up, Ellie,' I say, watching my father, who has stopped wiping the counter and is now simply holding onto the edges. 'Just shut up, all right?'

My father turns around and glowers at us. 'Honestly, girls, how old are you?'

'Well, I guess I'm forty-three,' Ellie begins.

'I wasn't looking for an answer,' my father says. 'My point is, you're too old to ruin a weekend like this. Must you always bicker?'

'Well Dad, it's not bickering,' Ellie says with a frowny smile. 'It's more a war, I'd say.'

These last words seem to kick my father in the face. Something goes slack. His eyes droop and darken in their sockets. When he finally speaks, his voice is low and husky, as though someone has unstrung his vocal chords.

'What is it about birthdays in this family, anyway?' he asks. 'Why can't anyone just turn forty-one and enjoy the goddamn day?'

It's a shocking thing for my father to say. Usually he's the one who sees the glass half full, who compliments the cook when the dish is burned, who all night long manages to keep his toe from catching the hole in the guestbed sheet.

'Dad,' I say.

'I didn't really mean war,' Ellie begins.

'You two,' our father says hoarsely. 'What do you do, sit around and plan how you can fuck up the weekend?'

Ellie and I look at each other, then quickly look away. This is the first time he's ever used that word in front of us. There is dried spittle in the corner of his mouth. He swallows the rest of his coffee, and sets the empty mug on the counter.

'I give up,' and he walks out.

We hear his footsteps in the hall, hear the front door open and close with a brassy click. After a few seconds Ellie goes to the sink, rinses his mug, and places it in the dishwasher. I sit down at the table and lay my head on my arms.

'Grampa said the F-word,' Rachel whispers.

'Come with me,' says Gabe. 'I've got something to show you,' and he leads her from the room, telling her something about parachutes.

For a long time, neither Ellie nor I speak. I

cannot raise my head. It occurs to me that my father has been dreading this birthday as much as I have; that he more than anyone else needed the weekend to be a success because at age seventy-one there is not a lot of time left to amend the customs of our family. How could I have missed this need of his? Am I forever just a daughter?

I hear my sister leave the sink. She turns on the ceiling fan and I feel the cool air on my neck, and then I realize it is not just cool air but Ellie's fingers, making me shiver, the way she used to when we were children, when we cracked imaginary eggs over each other's head. Her nails are long, and glide like coins through my hair.

'Blew that one, didn't I,' she says.

If I wanted, I could dig the knife in right now. I could say, You sure did, or Why do you always have to make that one extra jab, or Can't you see how old he is?

I say nothing, however. I sit there as still as a prayer, not moving or saying anything. She starts kneading my shoulders. After our mother died, when I was having trouble sleeping, Ellie would give me backrubs. It was something our mother had done when we were young, and Ellie seemed to have inherited the touch, kneading and stroking and pummeling my flesh. Afterward she always squeezed the nape of my neck, which caused me to tingle and shiver. Finally she bent over and kissed my hair, and told me that she loved me, and I believed it; and that was the right thing for me to do, because it was true.

'He's pretty fragile,' I say.

'I know.' Ellie combs her fingers through my hair. 'I'm not crazy,' she says. 'I'm not her.'

'Then quit acting like her,' I say into my elbow.

'It's habit.'

'So break it.'

'Right,' she says quietly.

'Why'd you do it?' I say. 'And why do you keep lying about it?'

'Because Dad doesn't need to know everything at his age. He's gone through enough shit. Oh, crap, it was a stupid thing to do. But I was so pissed. I still am. How can he leave me like this?'

For the first time this weekend, I feel as though what Ellie is saying comes from the heart, true and unadorned, with no defenses and no words added for shock value. And I see her now as scared, and rejected, and lonely, and hurt. I may have gone through my own turmoil this summer, when Gabe was living down in town, but Ellie has it hands down on this issue.

'One minute I loved him, and the next minute I hated him,' she says. 'Can I be honest? Like without you throwing my words back at me in court?'

My chest aches with regret.

'Try to imagine it,' she says. 'Your husband tells you he's leaving you. Now hey, things haven't been so great and you've even imagined saying it to him but it still hits you like a ton of bricks. He tells you there's somebody else. He tells you they haven't slept together yet, although you know that's a crock. You think of him comparing you to her, how maybe he was watching you a few nights back while you were sleeping, wondering how to break the news. You poor thing you.'

She digs with her thumbnail at the line of dirt where sink and counter meet. What she gets, she rolls together and flicks away, and then she digs some more.

'And your first reaction is to figure out a way to get back at him. Hurt him the way he hurt you. But guess what! There's no one in the picture for you! So what do you do? How do you hurt him?'

'Open a window.'

'It was just a threat. But I thought it would at least give him a good jolt of adrenaline,' Ellie says. 'Make him rethink what he meant to me. I should have known better.'

She lights a cigarette and blows the smoke up into the fan. 'Want to know how much I hated him? I hated him so much I imagined killing him. It's true. I mean it. I imagined killing him so that he couldn't be happy again. Can you believe that? Bad shit, huh?'

'Not so bad,' I say.

'Yeah, well. Fortunately, I didn't say that out loud to him. He'd have had a field day, as Mother would have said. And by the way, don't you go worrying about me murdering my husband. I just had a lucid moment. I just saw how someone could do it. It doesn't mean I'm going to do it. That's the thing about being wacko, you know. Everyone thinks you're going to actually do the things you talk about.'

There is something else I have to ask, not to be mean, but because I simply need to understand.

'Didn't you think about what it was like for Rachel, watching you do that?'

Ellie doesn't answer. I wait, hoping for something that will clarify everything — that she told Rachel it was just a joke, that she had a rope around her waist. But Ellie just rolls the tip of her cigarette against a plate, nudging off cold ashes. After a while she looks at me, briefly, and then looks back at her cigarette.

'I did,' she says, 'but I couldn't stop myself.' She grinds out her cigarette and places it on top of the small pile she has created over the course of the morning.

'Look, about the money,' she says. 'You guys really don't owe me anything, you know. Maybe you owe Wilson, since it came out of his account. But we're getting divorced, remember. So you don't owe me. And if Wilson's down ten grand, I don't think any of us are going to weep.'

I'm not sure if this is correct in terms of New York marital property law, but I don't think it matters, for our purposes. Gabe has an out.

'Hey Gabe,' Ellie yells. 'Gabe!'

When Gabe comes back into the kitchen, Ellie explains the shift in assets and obligations. Gabe looks dubious.

'Look, Gabe,' my sister says, 'if it'll make you feel better, give Rachel some hang gliding lessons when she's old enough. Take her camping. Find me a boyfriend. Get me some good dope to smoke. And speaking of in vitro, are you sure you

212

don't want those eggs?'

'We're sure,' I say. 'We're going to adopt.' I slip my arm around Gabe's waist. Somewhere out there, on the other side of the world, a lone sperm has won the race and cells are dividing. Tonight a zygote, tomorrow an embryo, and nine months from now a yawling bundle will be passed from one set of arms to another.

Ellie doesn't take this as any momentous announcement. 'Probably just as well, since I got a notice this summer that the power went down and the lab got a little hot. So the eggs are probably bad anyway. Oh well, out they go,' she says cheerfully.

I glance out the window to see my father bend over to give Rachel a foothold so she can hoist herself up into the lower branches of a pine. She looks at us and points up, nodding. Ellie shakes her head sternly. My father, whose rare bursts of anger do not dissolve quickly, doesn't look back. Again I think of how much he needed to go home with a good birthday under his belt.

Ellie gives a sharp rap on the kitchen window pane. Then another. Finally my father consents to turn around. Ellie points to Rachel, then to the ground, and we see him speaking to the girl, who wiggles about to settle herself on the lowest branch, face raised to the sun.

'Isabel,' Ellie says, her eyes locked on the scene outside the window. 'About what Dad said. We're just another normal family now, you know. And be honest. Even normal families can't always get together without some kind of time bomb.'

It's not clear to me whether she is talking about what has already happened, or whether there is more to come. In any case I don't like the reference to a time bomb. I remark that I could name a few such normal families, although the only ones I can think of are those on sit-coms.

'Well, maybe,' Ellie allows. 'But most of us come with a fuse sticking out. Somebody makes a toast and boom.'

'You weren't always this cynical,' I tell her.

'You think I'm cynical?' she asks, surprised.

'Well,' I say, 'well, yes, I do.'

'Trust me,' she says, turning back to the window. 'I'm not cynical. If I was, I would have jumped.'

20

It was Nana who had the hardest time at my mother's funeral. Who could blame her? She hadn't seen our mother for two years, and didn't know how much our mother had deteriorated. At least we were somewhat prepared. Nana had no clue.

Putting aside her fear of airplanes, she flew out with her nurse Sally for the funeral. I was shocked to see how much she'd aged. She'd shrunk, for one thing, and now stood no higher than my chin. No longer did she wear a tidy gray bun; instead, her white hair flew out in sketchy wisps, with pink scalp showing through. Her glasses were thick and square, her eyes cloudy and bluish, as though someone had put a drop of skim milk in each one.

The worst was her face. The stroke had paralyzed one side, and whenever she spoke of my mother, her good side got all contorted while her bad side stayed flat and indifferent. Her face represented the way I felt: devastated, on the one hand, that my mother was really, truly gone, and relieved, on the other, that we would no longer have to worry about the worst thing that could happen. It already had.

Nana and Sally set up quarters in our living room. I did not like this one bit. Although Sally neatly folded up the sofa bed every morning, Nana's little amber bottles of pills lay all around, along with tissue boxes and half-empty glasses of water. It was a constant reminder of eternal sickness and death, from which I had no escape.

There were no gifts this time, and Nana in her state didn't notice the ratty T-shirts Ellie and I were sleeping in, or the threadbare towels, or the chipped plates or the mismatched water glasses. She didn't say anything about the TV dinners and cans of soup, and never once mentioned Antoine's. Ellie and I spent much of the time buttering toast and brewing tea for her. My father told us in private he was proud of us for taking care of her. I accepted the compliment, though I simply wanted her to go home and die. I couldn't help recalling all the bowls of gluey oat-meal she'd cooked for us, how she always said no to the Trix, how she always tried to stand in for my mother. Now, cruelly, I saw her only as a surrogate once again, and not, as I should have, as an old and sickly woman who had flown across the country to bury her only child.

The day of the funeral started out smoothly. We had a job, which was to bury my mother, and everyone seemed to accept the unspoken assumption that raw emotion would interfere with the end result. I cleaned the kitchen and Ellie swept the porch and my father emptied all the waste-baskets. With Sally's help, Nana got herself dressed in a gray suit, an old one which, due to her weight loss, hung from her shoulders like a bad find at the thrift shop. But the fabric was still thick and woolly, the stitching intact. Nana had always shopped for quality.

'Farg!' she exclaimed. 'Farg unst!' holding out

her good arm so we could feel the fabric.

'Ongafu,' Nana said, gazing into the mirror with satisfaction.

The funeral was to be held at the small stone church right down our street, the same church where Nana so many years ago had found the minister so praiseworthy. At Nana's insistence we walked, with Nana leading the way, bent over her walker as she wobbled along. The rest of us followed, respectful of her slow pace, even when the walker's rubber-tipped feet kept catching on the raised root cracks, and she had to halt and give it an angry little hop to dislodge it and move on.

Not knowing the current minister very well, and not wanting to put a man of God in an uncomfortable position, my father had chosen not to disclose the details of my mother's death to him. But I could tell from the way he kept adjusting the collar of his robe that he knew everything. After a few brief words with my father, he led us down the aisle to the front pew, and one by one we all sat down.

At the foot of the pulpit lay my mother's casket. Its light, polished wood was the color of peanut butter, and at each end stood a bouquet of white chrysanthemums, the kind we used to see in Antoine's. The casket was closed. The night before, the funeral director had asked my father if he wanted an open casket. Perhaps the girls would like to see the body one more time, he suggested. Body! I thought, horrified. I didn't want to see my mother's body! I knew that my father had chosen a blue dress for her, and he'd laid a photograph on her chest, a picture of our family up at Paradise Lodge one summer day. I didn't want to see her lying there in a strange blue dress that I'd never seen her wear before, with her eyes closed and that makeupy look I'd heard about from one of my friends. I wanted to think of her as she was in the picture. Hair blowing in the wind. The hausfrau parka. The blinding snowfields in the background.

My father noticed the look on my face. No, he told the director. Closed will be fine.

Shortly after we sat down, the organ music stopped, and the minister began to speak. There was nobody in the church except our little group. The minister droned on about dust to dust and ashes to ashes, how the Lord giveth and the Lord taketh away, and although it was a pretty shabby service, I figured we'd all muddle through without anyone falling apart.

But just after the minister said his final amen, as he bowed his head and stepped down from the pulpit, Nana tipped her head back and began this long, melodic wail, fluid and cat-like, as though some endless ribbon of grief were being drawn from the depths of her heart. It was a sound from another continent, from another side of the world. Nobody could calm her — not my father, who reached over and held her hand, or Sally, who kept barking her name in a loud whisper.

I had dreaded something like this. Apart from my mother, our family didn't put on emotional shows. My father has always been a restrained man, and even in this most awful of circumstances, his display of grief was limited to that one awful cry as he cradled her lifeless head in the garage. Even Ellie and I kept our tears inside until after the lights were out, when we cried into our pillows. Nana's wail, on the other hand, came unleashed with a maternal fury I didn't think possible in a woman her age.

Then Ellie joined in. Same posture, same sound as Nana. It became a kind of absurd competition between the two of them, with my father looking on in frozen shock. I nudged Ellie, thinking she was doing it for show. But she didn't stop, and obviously I couldn't kick my ailing grandmother. As a last resort I leaned forward with my head between my knees and clasped my hands behind my neck and started humming one long note to drown out the sound.

Nobody heard the heavy church door close against itself. When I lifted my head, my father was gone. In their wailing, Nana and Ellie hadn't noticed, either. But Sally had, and she shot me a panicked look that told me she was thoroughly incapable of taking charge and it was all up to me. I could only stare back at her. We were supposed to go to the cemetery right after the service. How could we go without my father?

Leaving the wailing women behind, I hurried up the aisle, out of the church and into the misty spring air. I looked up and down the street, but saw no sign of my father. I raced home and ran all through the house. He was not there. I screamed his name. He did not answer.

Suddenly I thought: Why, he's gone and killed

himself too. I'm an orphan now. A suicide orphan.

And I knew where he'd done it.

With my heart slamming against my chest, I ran out the kitchen door to the garage. I hadn't been in there since the night it happened, and in fact I'd sworn to myself that I would never set foot in there again. But I had no choice. I envisioned my father hanging from a rope. Lying in a pool of blood. Slumped against the wall, with Nana's empty pill bottles scattered on the concrete floor.

With shaking hands, I turned the knob and pushed open the door.

Of course, if I'd stopped to think about it, the empty garage proved nothing. It certainly wasn't the only place my father might have killed himself. But I was so stuck on the idea that he'd only have done it where my mother had done it, that when I looked around the garage — and I looked twice, to make sure — and satisfied myself that it was empty, I felt giddy. I was not an orphan! There was someone left to take care of me! A thousand centuries now stretched before me, full of life and hope and all the blessedly boring mundanities this world can offer.

Eventually I found my father at the bottom of the forty-nine steps, with dripping fern fronds all around him. He must have heard me, but he didn't turn around. I touched his shoulder, and he reached up and hooked his fingers into mine. Then he cleared his throat, and took out a handkerchief, and blew his nose.

I sat down on the step above him. The wood was dark and slick, with streaks of green fungus. All around, daffodil shoots were poking up out of the rotted leaves. In another week their yellow blooms would spatter the hillside with light.

'Remember that day your mother pushed the Plymouth into the lake?' he asked, after a while.

I nodded.

'You know what I thought?'

'No.'

'Well, I thought, now she'll see how crazy she is, now she'll get some real help.'

'What do you mean, real help?'

'I guess I thought she'd start seeing her doctor more,' my father said. 'The funny thing is, she did, after we got back.'

'He didn't help her very much,' I said.

My father smiled ruefully. 'No, he didn't.'

'Then why'd she keep on going to him?' I asked. 'Why didn't she go to someone else?'

'She liked him,' my father said. 'She told me she was seeing all sorts of things in a new light. Nana, her father, growing up when she did. She said a lot of memories were coming back.'

'Did you ever talk to the doctor?'

'No,' my father said. 'He wouldn't talk to me. He didn't want to hear what I had to say.'

'Do you think she told him the truth?' I asked. 'Do you think she told him everything?'

'I don't know,' my father said. 'Your mother could be a flirt. She may indeed have left out a lot of things. I imagine she painted a very charming picture of herself.'

'Then he wasn't a very good doctor, was he?' I

said. 'He didn't even come to the funeral. What kind of a doctor doesn't come to the funeral?'

'He was all she had,' my father said.

'Well, he wasn't good enough,' I said bitterly. 'If he was any kind of good, she wouldn't be dead.' It struck me that this was a cruel thing to say to a man who had just lost his wife, who had tried to help and who in all likelihood was already holding himself responsible for a lot of things, including his failure to insist that she see another doctor. I wished I hadn't said it.

'I said some things to her,' I said thickly.

'What kind of things?'

'Mean things,' and I proceeded to tell him about the incident when she came into the bathroom during my bath. I left out the part about the Kotex; I simply couldn't bring myself to say the word in front of my father.

'And what did you say that was so mean?' he asked.

'I told her she was a bad mother.'

My father looked at me with hollow, aching eyes. For a minute I thought he was going to hold me responsible for everything. But then he reached up and tucked a strand of hair behind my ears.

'Oh, that,' he said. 'Yes, she told me.' I was puzzled to hear this until I recalled the sound of water running in the bathtub that night, and their voices behind the closed door. 'She knew you didn't mean it,' he said.

'How do you know?'

'She told me.'

'She lied, then,' I said stubbornly.

'It's possible,' my father said, 'but I don't think so. Besides, we all said some mean things to her. You certainly weren't the only one. You want to hear what I told her once?'

I waited.

'I told her that if she didn't stop all her strange behavior, I would leave her, and take you and Ellie with me, and she would never see you girls again.'

'You told her that?'

'I didn't mean it,' my father said. 'And she knew I wouldn't leave. But I wanted to shake her up. I thought if I threatened her, she'd change.'

I unrolled a fiddlehead that was poking up through the fronds of a fern. When I let go, it coiled back into itself, looser now, ruined.

'Dad?'

'What's that, honey?'

'Did it hurt?'

'Did what hurt?'

'Dying. The way she did it.'

'No,' my father said quietly, 'it didn't hurt.'

'Did she know she was dying?'

'I imagine she did, Izzy.'

'Do you think she thought of turning off the engine at the last minute?'

'I don't know, Isabel,' my father said. 'I'll never know.'

'I think she was going to, but forgot,' I said. 'Do you think that's possible?'

'Yes,' he said. 'It's certainly possible.'

I considered this theory; like other people's notions of heaven, I knew it was going to get me through the coming weeks and months.

'What'll happen to the garage now?' I asked.

'Oh, I think we'll probably tear it down,' my father said.

I was grateful to hear this. Naturally, I wanted to avoid the memories; but, recalling my panicked state a few minutes ago, I also wanted to make sure there were no deadly lures to tempt my father.

'Yes,' my father said, 'it's old, and the wood's rotting. We should have torn it down a long time ago.'

★　★　★

After the burial, we all went home to an empty house. I had some preconceived notions of what this time should be like. My friend's grandmother had died the year before, and after the funeral their house was full of people talking, laughing, eating and drinking. Our house was nothing like that. My father opened up a couple of cans of Dinty Moore. Nana, exhausted from wailing, fell asleep on the sofa. The rest of us watched Walter Cronkite.

It was Ellie who turned things around. An ad for dog food came on. Remember Wally? Ellie said. Remember how she farted? Remember that time she stuck her nose into the principal's crotch? My father hadn't heard that story, and he smiled when she told it, he even laughed, Sally too, and soon all of us were laughing so hard that tears came again. Only now they came from the light, and not from the dark, and although it was a just tiny speck of light, and not very bright, it made me feel as though things would settle down, and our lives might, one day, turn out as normal as anybody's.

21

Family weekends can draw you into a time warp. The hours either fly by or they drag to a standstill, depending on how everyone's getting along. Last night everything slowed down almost to a stop, such that I now find myself remembering each word that was said. *If she loved us, she never would have left us . . . So, what, you're saying I'm a bad mother?* Parts of the morning, too, have clotted into a collection of freeze-frame images. Ellie tightening the sash of her bathrobe. Rachel touching her stitches. My father walking out on Ellie and me.

But now that everyone seems to have come right out and articulated every single thought and opinion that's occurred to him or her during the last twenty-eight years, time shifts gears, and the moments blur. Rachel comes in all pitchy from the pine tree and my father disappears for a long shower and someone makes a fresh pot of coffee; second breakfasts turn into nibbly lunches that turn into my father nodding off on the sofa while Ellie scrubs at Rachel's pitch with nail polish remover and wonders aloud whether Gabe and his brother fought the way she and I did, and whether they made their peace before he went off to Vietnam. I don't know, I told her. Don't ask, though.

All too soon it is time for people to leave. At three o'clock my father appears in the living room, packed, combed, tucked, and belted. He has not completely recovered. I can tell this by the way he works his tongue over his gums before he says goodbye, and it makes me wish that Suzanne were going to be there for him when he gets home. Some people you can fight to the eyeballs in front of. My father is not one of them.

I walk with him out to the Land Cruiser. On the passenger seat lies his Hertz map, with his route highlighted in yellow. Once again I think back to my mother and our trips in the Plymouth, when we had neither map nor food nor change of clothes, when we just got in the car and drove, the three of us stopping for dinner at a pancake house where my mother would drink a martini and Ellie and I would fight over the jukebox selections and we might or might not call our father with our whereabouts, depending on my mother's level of empathy for his concern. My father plans to have his kayak shipped at a later time, so for now the two boats lie propped against the garage, side by side. He gets into the driver's seat, closes the door, and rolls down the window. For a moment, neither of us speak. He keeps his hands on the steering wheel and stares out the front window.

Finally he says, gruffly, 'She's your sister, you know. The two of you are going to need each other when I'm gone. Don't fight so much. It kills me to hear you talk that way.'

The sound of the Eagles' 'Hotel California' comes from the living room. Through the sliding door I see a shadow glide by, a glimmer of limbs,

227

a smaller figure turning cart-wheels.

'Dad,' I say, my voice starting to crack, 'Daddy, I still miss her.'

He doesn't need to ask. 'We all do,' he says. 'But love what you have. You have a lot to love.'

Since yesterday I have been feeling as though large chunks of time keep slipping through my fingers. But this particular moment — my father's words, his reaching out one last time to squeeze my hand before adjusting the mirror and turning the ignition — this particular moment is as solid and enduring as the moon.

He backs out of the driveway. He gives a wave. I wave back, and he drives off.

★   ★   ★

Back upstairs Ellie and Rachel are themselves trying to get ready to depart, rushing about in a flurry of lost bracelets, missing socks, and numerous checks under the bed. We both seem cognizant of the fact that much remains unresolved; that a trial lies ahead, with depositions, interrogatories, and child psychologists on both sides. But we are loathe to give up the safety of our truce in a quest for commitments. In fact, in the final moments Ellie seems mostly concerned with getting her Yankees' cap just right. Standing on the deck, with her bags packed and Rachel's bladder as empty as it will ever be, she slaps the hat repeatedly and rolls the brim this way and that before finally putting it on. The two of them lumber down the steps with their lumpy duffels swinging from side to side; they drop them in the trunk and there is one last round of quick hugs and then they, too, are gone.

After a long time my husband comes out on the deck.

'Izzy? Are you coming up?'

★ ★ ★

That night Gabe takes me out to dinner at a streetside café down in town. Over a basket of bread and a bowl of olive oil, he asks me if I had a good weekend.

'Gabe,' I say, 'don't ask dumb questions.'

We must be back on track, because I feel free to be as bitchy as I want right now.

'Okay, so there were a few blow-ups,' he says. 'But don't you think that all things considered, it went pretty well?'

'What do I do about Wilson?'

'Do you have to decide tonight?'

'No.'

'Then for right now you don't do anything about Wilson.'

I can't let go of the issue. 'Say I testify. Say he gets custody. She'd be devastated.'

'What does that mean?'

'She'd jump.'

'She wouldn't jump.'

'Yes she would. And it'd be my fault.'

'No it wouldn't, Isabel,' Gabe says quietly. 'It'd be her own fault.'

I want very much to believe him, to have learned a lesson from my mother's death.

'Look, your father and I talked about this. No one can know what's ever going to happen. You do what you can to make things work out right, and maybe they will. But she's a grown woman,' he says. 'She makes her own choices. You can't keep torturing yourself, when she's the one in charge.'

'That makes perfect sense — let her do what she wants — until you add Rachel to the picture.'

'Well, cross that bridge when you have more information,' Gabe says.

This is my father's famous 'sleep on it and things will fall into place in the morning' formula. It's essentially an avoidance technique, but hearing it from Gabe makes me feel as though I have really, truly married the right man.

Gabe pauses for a moment, then reaches into his pocket. 'Here,' and he hands me a small package. 'Your birthday present.'

It's jewelry, I can tell from the size of the box, and I think, hey, nothing wrong with jewelry. But I am wrong. When I unwrap the box and lift the cover, I find a pile of brown seeds and shriveled red berries on a bed of cotton batting.

'Seeds,' I say, waiting.

'Not just seeds,' he says. 'Tree seeds. Look,' and he pokes them about. 'Here's a pine tree seed. Here's a blue spruce. Here's a crabapple, and let's see, this is a lilac. I thought it was time to fix up the yard. See this berry? You know what it is? It's a madrona berry,' he says proudly. 'I got your father to bring it. You're always talking about the madrona trees in Seattle. What the heck is a madrona tree, anyway? Not that I can promise anything, since the climate conditions are a little different here.'

'Do people even grow trees from seed these days?'

'I don't think so. We'll get the root-balled things.' Suddenly he looks shy. 'I just thought it was kind of an original way to put the idea in a box.'

'Gabe,' I say, leaning across the table to kiss him, 'thank you. That is a very cool thing to give me.'

'I mean, I was looking around this weekend,' he continues. 'Our yard looks so empty. It is a dog pen. We need plants. We need flowers. We need leaves turning color in the fall.'

'We need to go to New Hampshire sometime,' I say.

'We need to go everywhere,' my husband says.

★　★　★

I am straightening up in the guest room, stripping the beds, collecting cups, when my eye catches a small pile of colored glass on the floor between bed and nightstand. I bend down and pick it up. It is my mother's hula skirt bracelet, the one she used to wear on road trips. I hold it up to the light and stretch the chain. The dangling glass pipes sparkle with their ruby reds, their bottle greens and clear, cobalt blues.

This must be what Ellie was searching for, before she left today. I didn't even know she had it. In fact, even though we used to fight over who

231

would inherit it, the bracelet dropped off my radar screen many, many years ago. One-handedly I clasp its chain around my left wrist. The tiny glass pipes feel cool against my skin. I raise my arm and twist it back and forth, letting the pipes do their hula dance against my arm, and I can see, once more, my mother's wrist upon the steering wheel, her flattened pack of Winstons on the seat, her red scarf rising behind her in the wind.

For some reason, knowing that Ellie kept the bracelet all these years, knowing that a piece of costume jewelry can hold such meaning for an unsentimental person like Ellie — knowing this nurtures a small seed of trust within me. Complete trust? In my sister? No. And I probably won't ever stop worrying. But I can pretend to believe. Call it denial, call it a lie, call it whatever. But it seems that a little denial here and there isn't a bad thing, if it lets you hope, and if it helps other people keep their lives stitched together when they might need it, to get to a better place. Wilma's probably denying like hell these days.

It makes me think that maybe my mother's main problem near the end was that she lost this ability to deny, or lie. This in turn would have forced her to wake up to her entire litany of terrifying truths every morning. All this time I've thought that her lying was part of her illness. Now I see that it was part of her survival plan, that when she stopped lying — for whatever reason — she found herself smack up against a wall of hopelessness.

And standing here in the guest room, looking at the photograph of my mother at the top of the forty-nine steps, I want to tell her that I'm sorry she stopped lying. Crazy or not, sometimes all of us have to keep on deceiving ourselves, because who's to say what is true, and what is not.

★　★　★

The first thing I do at the office on Monday morning is call Wilma to make sure she knows she can call me if something comes up. Tracy answers. I tell her I spoke with her mother on Saturday, and I was sorry to hear that she was sick.

'Thank you,' Tracy says in a small voice. I've seen her, and know how overweight she is, and can't quite picture how a little black mole can threaten such a tremendous body.

'When do you start treatment?' I ask.

'I don't know.' With each word, her voice grows smaller.

'Don't be frightened,' I say. 'You'll get through.'

'I don't want my little girl to be left all alone,' she whispers.

What do I say? I don't know that her little girl won't be left all alone. I can lie to myself, but not to others.

'Is your mother home?' I ask.

'No. She's gone to get groceries.'

'Could you have her call me?'

'Sure.'

'Tracy?'

'What?'

'It'll be all right,' I offer.

'Thanks,' she says.

We hang up, and I set Wilma's file on my credenza. I think of how little comfort I can offer Tracy. I wonder if indeed her daughter Erin will be what keeps her going. I also wonder what information Tracy has received about her condition. At a time like this my mother would have gone to the library and read up on the medical literature and scared herself shitless. I hope Tracy can be more rational.

I'd planned on calling Wilson next to find out more about Ellie's behavior of late. But I don't feel like talking to Wilson right now. Instead, I open my bottom desk drawer and take out the Yellow Pages. I flip to 'Adoption.' There are three pages of listings. Some of the larger ads are designed in shades of pink and light blue, with pictures of butterflies, or storks, or teddy bears. They boast of babies to be gotten from Russia, China, Romania, Korea, Thailand, and Ecuador. There are ads for Christian solutions and Jewish solutions, open and closed, designated, interstate, all expenses paid. There are websites. There are 1-800 numbers. There is even an agency right down at the bottom of the hill here in town.

I had no idea.

Epilogue

(One year later)

This year for my forty-second birthday, Gabe gives me one of those little stands that converts my road bike into a stationary bike, so I can work out in our living room. He also gives me a double-seater BabyJogger, with padded handles and full suspension and dirt-bike tires guaranteed to take the most active parents on all types of trail. I kid him that the BabyJogger is for him as much as me, but he denies it. For *his* birthday, he tells me, he wants matching baby backpacks, now that the girls' heads aren't flopping all over the place, his goal being to get our family of four up to the Continental Divide before the Forest Service closes off the road to Brainard Lake for the winter.

It's been a quiet birthday. The only thing I didn't get that I wished for is that book on solving your child's sleep problems. Actually, what I really need is a book on solving my own sleep problems, since I'm the one who can't fall asleep though the twins are now sleeping through the night. It's a case of conditioning. You get woken up five or six times a night for three months running, it's hard to believe you're not going to get woken up again.

Nobody can explain it, not to my satisfaction. Last year, about five weeks after my birthday, I got the flu. I fell asleep at my desk. I fainted in court. When the flu didn't go away I became convinced I had cancer and lined up all sorts of appointments, but it was during my first one, with my plain old OB/Gyn, that she stuck her whole entire arm up inside me and promptly informed me I was pregnant.

I got mad. She said it wasn't any joke. She'd never felt a more pregnant cervix than mine. When the tests came back confirming the diagnosis, I had to apologize, although privately I kept thinking it was a joke until an ultrasound at twelve weeks showed not one but two beating hearts, two darkened blurs that to my untrained eye looked like something you might see if you opened your eyes in pond water.

My doctor just shrugs. Who knows how it happened? she asks. Who cares?

My sleep deprivation worries Ellie. She arrived a few days ago and said the bags under my eyes made me look like a torture victim. There's no one like your sister to be frank. I said I thought I looked no worse and no better than any other mother of three-month-old twins, but she diagnosed a B-vitamin deficiency, went down to a natural foods store, and came back with a shopping bag of pills and juices and salves and lotions, essential oils for the bath, scented candles and a rare African root cream for my nipples.

There are questions I would like to ask my mother. How long were your labors? Did Ellie or I have colic? Did you have postpartum night sweats? How often did you reach the point of exhaustion where you wanted to throw the kid against the wall? And how often did you close your eyes and put your cheek against mine, or Ellie's, and wish for only good things to happen to us, for the next hundred million years?

Ellie's divorce came through last week, which is why she is out here visiting me now. I never did have to take sides, because she and Wilson managed to agree upon joint custody, which almost led me to start believing in God, just so I could have someone to thank in the middle of the night.

Not that everything has gone smoothly for them. Any peace is a fragile peace. Last summer Wilson was finally charged with tax evasion, and fined more money than Gabe and I earn in a year. The penalty bothers Ellie far less than the fact that he and his new girlfriend flaunt their affection in front of Rachel.

For her part, Ellie switched medications. This constituted a good-faith effort, but the new medications made her manic, and she ended up going out and buying new furniture and new kitchen cabinets and even a new car. It was a white Mercedes, big enough to take Rachel on long road trips from New York up into the White Mountains of New Hampshire, where she planned to climb every peak over five thousand feet and see if it was true that you could see from one state to another, like our mother claimed. I pointed out to Ellie that she'd never climbed a mountain in her life, and she just said what could be difficult about putting one foot in front of the other? Fortunately her doctor adjusted her meds, and she was able to return most of the furniture and cancel the cabinet order, although she kept the car, which she uses to drive Rachel and her friends out to Long Island every once in a while.

She's doing just fine, she maintains, except for the fucking hot flashes.

Me, I'm not worrying about perimenopause right now. I'm content these days with a solid three-hour block of sleep. Most of the time I sit and feed the girls. I've set up a nursing station in the living room, one whole sofa filled with dozens of downy pillows that I can use to prop one or both babies to my breasts and have my hands free to read or write. Which I never do. Instead I sit there staring out the window like someone with an IQ of about fifty. Sometimes the strangest memories come back. Car trips, or holidays, or coloring at the kitchen table while my mother scrubs her empty jars. They all float by.

One memory keeps reappearing. A year after my mother's death, when I was in the eighth grade, I won a writing award. My teacher wanted me to read the piece at an all-school assembly. I was terrified. As I walked onto the stage, I could hear Niagara Falls all around me, and thought I would faint.

Then, clutching the podium, I saw my mother. She was sitting right in the middle of the audience. She'd knotted her blue scarf neatly under her chin, and was wearing her red cat's-eye sunglasses. She smiled at me, and as soon as she did, the waterfall stopped. I cleared my throat and began to read. Every time I looked up, there she was, smiling. When I finished, the gymnasium rang with a hollow silence, until my mother herself stood up and began to clap, just like she'd done so many years ago after my Pilgrim play. As the rest of the audience burst into applause, I smiled back. She took off her glasses, folded them, and tucked them into her pocket, and then she smiled once more and was gone.

I like to remember her that way.

Acknowledgments

Special thanks to my editor, Pat Walsh, for believing in this book. Also, because a good portion was written during my arts-in-education residencies, a heartfelt thanks to everyone at Young Audiences, Inc.; the Colorado Council for the Arts; and the teachers, students, and staff at my sponsoring schools.

On a personal note, I am deeply grateful to Laura Uhls, Lisa Halperin, MD, and Richard Suddath, MD, for their continuing comments on the manuscript. And I could never have begun, sustained, or finished the book without the love, support, and never-ending criticism from my husband, Pierre Schlag.

A mountain of blessings for my beloved sisters.

We do hope that you have enjoyed reading this large print book.

Did you know that all of our titles are available for purchase?

We publish a wide range of high quality large print books including:
Romances, Mysteries, Classics
General Fiction
Non Fiction and Westerns

Special interest titles available in large print are:
The Little Oxford Dictionary
Music Book
Song Book
Hymn Book
Service Book

Also available from us courtesy of Oxford University Press:
Young Readers' Dictionary
(large print edition)
Young Readers' Thesaurus
(large print edition)

For further information or a free brochure, please contact us at:
Ulverscroft Large Print Books Ltd.,
The Green, Bradgate Road, Anstey,
Leicester, LE7 7FU, England.
Tel: (00 44) 0116 236 4325
Fax: (00 44) 0116 234 0205

Other titles published by
The House of Ulverscroft:

THE ABORTIONIST'S DAUGHTER

Elisabeth Hyde

Living in a small town in Colorado, nineteen-year-old university student Megan Thompson is beautiful, cool, and sexy — the kind of girl boys fall in love with. She's steered clear of family life since the death of her younger brother . . . until the day she hears her mother, Diana, has been found floating face down in their swimming pool. Diana, as Director of the Center for Reproductive Choice, was a national figure who inspired passions — and made enemies. Detective Huck Berlin is brought in to investigate when it becomes clear that Diana was murdered. Several people had quarrelled with Diana on that fateful day, including her husband Frank, and her wayward child. Now father and daughter are thrown together in an unexpected twist of family life.

A GOLDEN AGE

Tahmima Anam

Rehana Haque is throwing a party in the rose-filled garden of the house she has built, while beyond her doorstep the city is buzzing with excitement after the recent elections. None of the guests at Rehana's party can foresee what will happen in the days and months that follow. For this is East Pakistan in 1971, a country on the brink of war. And this family's life is about to change for ever. Set against the backdrop of the Bangladesh War of Independence, *A Golden Age* is a story of passion and revolution, of hope, faith and unexpected heroism.

MORAL DISORDER

Margaret Atwood

Moral Disorder is a collection of eleven stories, snapshots tracing the course of a life, and the lives intertwined with it . . . The first story is set in the present, as a couple no longer young situate themselves in a world no longer safe. Then the narrative switches time, as the central character moves through childhood and adolescence. We follow her into young adulthood, through a complex relationship, and the heartbreaking old age of parents, but circle back to childhood again, to complete the cycle. By turns funny, moving, lyrical, incisive, tragic, earthy, shocking and deeply personal, *Moral Disorder* displays Atwood's celebrated storytelling gifts and inimitable style to their best advantage.

OUT OF THE BLUE

Charlotte Bingham

Florence Fontaine is recovering from a family tragedy when she discovers a young man asleep in her guest cottage at the Old Rectory. She offers him breakfast, only to rue the day as she finds herself caught up in the resulting drama of his life. Florence's young and beautiful daughter, Amadea, is suspicious of Edward, fearing that he might be a fraud. Florence enlists friends and neighbours to help discover who he might be. United in their quest, their dedication to help the young man takes Florence and Amadea on an adventure that takes them into many pasts. In doing so they are finally able to put tragedy behind them, repair their once disjointed lives, and embrace a new and happy future.

THE INCONSTANT HUSBAND

Susan Barrett

When Patrick McKinley steps into Rose Seaton's life, her heart finds its target. However, this bohemian artist is not the suitor for whom she was groomed: her father demands a Yorkshire son-in-law, with a talent for manufacturing, for his ironworks. What Rose wants is more exciting and dangerous, and Patrick soon ensnares her at a ball to celebrate Queen Victoria's diamond jubilee. But Patrick, for all his charm, is also broke and evasive and his strategies lead Rose into harm and scandal. Then, to indulge his pursuit of artistic utopias, they journey across Europe where Rose meets the other players in Patrick's life. She begins to grasp what it means to be a wife and a mother — and to question her role as a muse.